Contents

I think I'm falling

So slowly

That I didn't even know

I'd lost my balance

But it's too late now

And the ground is rushing towards me

I've got nothing to hold on to

And no one around

To help me up.

S C Hughes

Stay Forever

My name is Honey, I'm sixteen years old and I am in love.

Love, a small simple four-letter word that is powerful enough to change the course of the world. Yet words, for all their power, are not enough to encompass everything I feel for him. His name is Azra and he is my world, when I breathe, I breathe him, when I smile, it's because I'm thinking of him, and when I laugh, yup you guessed it…

Azra is 5'9", has dark brown eyes, black hair that falls almost perfectly across his forehead in an effortless sort of way and is drop dead gorgeous.

I know what you're wondering, "does he feel the same way about me?" YES. Yes, he does. Most of you are going to roll your eyes and tune out right there, but I hope that some of you will stick around.

A New Year

Back to school tomorrow, though I'm not exactly sure how I feel about that. Annoyed about having to start lessons again, I guess. Not that I don't like studying, I love it. I've always enjoyed learning new things, from as far back as I can remember I've been a bit of a bookworm. The reason I'm annoyed is because I won't be able to spend as much time with Azra. We are in the same year, but I don't have any lessons with him, unlike my best friend Carol, who does. Then again I'm a bit conflicted as to whether this is a good thing or not, because I'm sure as hell not going to be paying any attention to a teacher with Azra in the room. Not to say that I didn't just spend almost every single day of the summer holidays with him, it just seemed to be over so fast.

Stupid alarm, just when my dream was getting interesting. I smile as I lie back and try to remember as much detail of it as possible.

"Honey get down here, breakfast is ready and you don't want to be late on your first day back," yelled mum from downstairs.

"Coming ma," I call out and push the covers back. After a long stretch and a last look at my warm comfy bed I head to the bathroom for a shower.

About forty-five minutes later I walk down the stairs and mum filled a plate as I take a seat at the dining table.

"Thanks ma," I gave her a big grin and pulled it towards me.

Scrambled eggs, toast and a cup of tea. Breakfast of champions.

"Looking forward to starting a new year?" Mum asked, taking a seat opposite me.

I give a shrug. "Yes and no," I reply between mouthfuls.

Mum laughed. "Worried you won't have as much time to spend with Azra?"

"Right on the money ma," I tell her with a little laugh of my own. "Anyway, gotta go, I'll see you later."

School is about a twenty-minute walk away and I enjoy the stroll. I normally leave about ten minutes earlier than I need to so that I can take my time, as I don't like being late. I've made this journey so often now that I can do it with my eyes closed, and when I turn the last corner it's possible to navigate by the noise alone. Today is even louder since it's the start of a new year.

My first lesson is history, which is great because I love it. I'm not exactly sure what I wanna do after I finish school, but I will definitely be looking at something in that direction for the next couple of years.

"Honey, hey Hon. Over here," called a voice from behind me.

That's Carol, we are so different that sometimes I wonder just how we became friends. Carol is loud, sometimes crude, always laughing, with guys as easily as she does with girls and doesn't care a damn what anyone says about her. Not that anyone actually says anything bad because she seems to fit in with just about everyone. Which is just one of the many things that I admire about her. Carol is taller than me, has long black hair and looks older, which is a bit annoying.

I'm exactly the opposite of Carol in so many ways and yet from the moment we met, pretty much on the first day of school we just clicked, and never looked back. We have been through it all together. We've argued, screamed at, laughed and cried together and not once have I ever doubted her or our friendship.

"Did he have to keep you to himself the whole summer?" Carol pouted, catching up to me. "I hardly got to see you at all."

"What are you talking about, we saw each other loads," I reply with a grin.

"Are you kidding me I barely saw you once or twice a week… Oh my God what's that, it's gorgeous". Carol pointed to my necklace wide eyed. Which she then grabbed and began to inspect extremely closely. Rather than have it torn off my neck I took a step towards her. The necklace in question is a silver chain with a crystal about an inch long, a centimetre wide in the middle and tapering to a point at both ends.

"He gave it to you didn't he? Right spill it. I want to know everything."

I blush just thinking about it. "Come on," I giggle, pulling her into a corner.

"Azra gave it to me as a birthday present last week," I whisper even though no one is actually paying any attention to us. "He took me to the top of the hill at the weekend and we were laying on a blanket looking at the sky, talking about school. You know, stuff like what we're gonna do after. It was a perfectly clear night…you should have seen it Carol, I've never seen so many stars before. We stared at them for a while then he turned to me and said…"

"You mean the world to me you know, and I would give you the stars themselves if I could". He reached up to the sky and grabbed something, and when he brought his hand back he was holding the necklace with the pendant in the middle of his palm.

Carol mimicked putting a finger down her throat. "You know that I'm not really one for the mushy stuff". She groaned. "Anyway… then what happened"? Her wide eyes betraying her curiosity.

"When he was putting it around my neck he whispered, there's a piece of my heart in that jewel. It's a fragile little thing and easily broken so you have to be gentle with it."

"I promise I'll never break it, and guard it with my life," I whisper back and he smiled as he ran his fingers through my hair then leant forward, I do the same without even realizing that I have.

When our lips meet it's like touching a live wire and a shock runs through my entire body, images tumble through my mind and become a white glare. His hand is on my waist now and he pulled me closer, I don't remember putting my arms around him, but my nails are digging into his back as I crush him against me. I can feel his chest against mine and my heart is like a jackhammer against my ribs. There's a roaring in my ears, I can't breathe, I…

"HON, hey Hon you zoned out there for a second." Carol waved a hand in front of my face. "He put it around your neck and…?"

"He kissed me," I reply, looking away. I'm breathing faster and my face feels hot, I know that I must be as red as a beetroot and Carol looked at me with a frown.

"Nice," she finally said with a smirk. "So, what happened then?"

"What do mean?" I asked, looking back at her.

"Oh come on Honey, you know exactly what I mean. What, do I have to spell it out for you?"

"Jeez Carol." I gasp. "No, we didn't. Besides, you know what my parents are like, especially my dad. If he even thought that I slept with a guy I probably won't see daylight again till I'm 21, if ever. And I don't even want to think about what he would do to Azra."

Don't get me wrong I love my parents and I know that they love me, but when you're brought up a certain way unspoken rules seem to get ingrained into your very cells. When I'm told to do something by them, I do it immediately. I would never dare argue with either of my parents, and even though I know that neither of them will ever hit me, I still get scared when I'm told off.

"Fine Miss Prim and Proper," Carol chuckled. "But it must have been some kiss to get that reaction from you. Although if I was in your place, after all that I would have definitely been curious to see where it might lead. I'm surprised he didn't jump on you right there."

"He's not like that," I reply, shocked. "We've been together for almost five months now and not once has he ever... Anyway come on," I grab Carol's hand and pull her along behind me. "Class is about to start, and I don't want to be late for my first lesson."

Azra looked at the clock on the wall again, and started counting down the last few seconds, when the bell for recess finally rang there was a stampede for the door.

Azra didn't like crowds, so he sat and waited for the rush to clear, the teacher was still talking about an assignment, but he needn't have bothered as no one was really listening anymore. Even Azra had zoned him out as he finally got up and headed to the exit.

Azra heard what the teacher had said the first time and had an excellent memory. It's so good that he only needed to read or hear something once to be able to recall it almost perfectly, what some would call a photographic memory.

He also has what his maths teacher calls an "amazing aptitude for numbers". Though he's not exactly sure what's so amazing about it. It came as a bit of a surprise when he realised that not everyone saw figures the same way that he did. Azra can spot trends and discrepancies as soon as he looked at a set of numbers. Sudoku is a breeze and he can finish even the "expert" level in seconds.

As soon as Azra stepped out of the door it felt like walking into a wall of sound. Anyone who has walked a school hall will know exactly what it's like. There's so much noise that you have to shout to be heard, which just adds to the volume.

Azra saw her as soon as he turned the corner and the smile that lit up her face when their eyes met just drowned out every bit of sound. Clichés about how beautiful she is tumble through his head, but nothing came even close to do her justice. Honey, named for the colour of her hair, which is golden blond and glows like it catches the sunlight, even when she's indoors. As the two of them walk towards each other their smiles get wider and their steps quicken.

"Hey." Azra grinned, taking Honey's hand and looked into her eyes which were light grey and sparkling, like starlight reflecting off an ocean of silver. He used to wonder what people meant when they said that someone has beautiful eyes, having never really taken much notice of a girl's eyes before, apart from the different colours that is. That was before meeting Honey, now he wondered yet again how he could have been so blind. Everything about her eyes draw him deeper in, from the length of her lashes to the curve of her brow. From the way her eyes light up, to the multitude of expressions that dance across them. And that's just the start Azra thought, he could go on forever thinking about Honeys eyes.

They talk about the morning while walking towards the cafeteria for lunch. Surprisingly they both have the same thing, sausage and mash with carrots, peas and a bit of gravy on the side.

Carol is sitting opposite Azra chatting away, but the only thing that's on his mind at that moment is that Honey's knee was lightly resting against his under the table.

Carol seemed to have left at some point and Azra wondered absent-mindedly when she did. They take the empty plates to the dirty pile and head towards the exit, there's an old tree in one of the far corners of the school grounds that they usually spend their break under, and the two of them slowly walk towards it now.

Azra joined the school about halfway through the previous term, and from the moment he saw Honey he was absolutely smitten. His mind drifted back on the crushes he's had on girls. Girls that he'd wanted to ask out and girls that he had. But not once had he ever felt anything like this before. It took him over a month to work up the courage to talk to Honey and finally ask her out, in what was one of the most nervous moments of his life. And she said yes straight away. Honey didn't hesitate or play hard to get like some girls do, especially the pretty ones.

Honey, the first time Azra said her name out loud it sounded funny, it felt weird, almost too personal. Like something a married couple would call each other. But he got used to it pretty quickly and now he seemed to randomly say it under his breath at the oddest moments, and there's always a smile on his face whenever he does.

"C'mon lovebirds, playtimes over and we need to get to class," Carol called, walking up.

Has it been an hour already? Honey thought, watching Azra getting up.

Carol grabbed Azra's hand and pulled him to his feet.

"Don't worry Hon I'll protect him from all the bad girls out there," Carol said with a wink towards me then linked her arm around Azra's.

I feel a pang of jealousy even though I know that she's not interested in Azra like that. Carol prefers the bad boys. Anyone in a leather jacket and she turns to stare, especially if he's wearing a white t-shirt underneath. Don't even mention a bike around her. I trust Carol with my life, and more importantly I trust her with my boyfriend. The jealousy turns to pride when I see Azra pull his hand away. They have a class together so I watch them for a moment before heading off to my own. Azra turned and gave me a smile before going through the doors.

The next few hours pass pretty quickly, I spend half my time paying attention in class and the other half daydreaming about Azra. Ok fine, its closer to all my attention being on him and just a few snippets of what the teachers are saying actually make it through to my brain. I doubt I'll miss much as we normally spend the first days or so going over what we studied towards the end of last term.

When the last bell sounds I make a dash for the doors with the rest of the class. Azra is at the front doors of the school, and he started walking towards me as soon as he saw me. I reached out and he took my hand as we headed out of the building.

“Here, let me take your bag.” Azra offered, reaching towards my shoulder.

“It’s ok, I can manage,” I reply with a grin. Some girls hand their bags over as soon as they see their boyfriend, like it’s part of the job description for the boy to carry it, some even pull out their phone and start texting as soon as they do. I don’t like that, it’s not that I'm into women’s lib or anything it’s just that he has his own bag, and I don’t want him to have to carry mine as well when I can easily do it myself.

While we walk back to my place we chat about our first day, with a comment here or there about homework. There are a few moments of silence, but it’s comfortable enough that neither of us feel the need to fill it. There’s a small lawn in front of my house with three steps leading up to the porch and a large wooden bench to the right of the front door, and Azra jumped over all three to land in front of the door.

“Ma I'm home,” I call when we walk in. There’s no answer, meaning that she isn’t back yet. Mum is a receptionist and she’s usually back the same time as me but can sometimes turn up about ten or twenty minutes after. It depends on what time she leaves the office, or if she does any shopping. It looks like we get a few minutes to ourselves today.

“You want anything?” I ask Azra when I open the fridge.

“Whatever you’re getting for yourself is fine.”

I take out two colas and we head up to my room. There was quite a heated discussion when I told my parents that I had a steady boyfriend. Dad’s immediate response was “no boys in your room,” but mum said that was too harsh. After a lot back and forth between them it was agreed that I had to leave my door open when Azra was here, and that he had to leave by 6.30 at the latest as we normally sit down for dinner at about 7 o’clock. Dad wasn’t very happy when he agreed to all this, but mum was quite adamant.

One of the conditions is that I had to promise them I wouldn't go to Azra's place. His parents Adam and Susan travel a lot and he has a guardian who lives in the apartment beside his. Which basically means that he's mostly alone, and dad doesn't trust us to be alone in his apartment together. I've been there a couple of times when we first started dating and it's really cool. There's a concierge at the entrance of his building and a killer view from his balcony.

I've kept my word on this and never been back since. I'm a really bad liar and find it uncomfortable to do so. I fidget a lot and can't even look at the person, never mind looking them in the eye. And lying about something when I've made a promise, especially to my parents is a definite no no. Azra has been really supportive of it, he said that I'm welcome to come over whenever I want, but he hasn't actually asked me back since.

It's a bit strange because when I was little it was always my father I went to whenever I needed anything. He would be the one to put a plaster on my knee or finger, wipe away any tears while whispering an encouraging word in my ear. A hug or a kiss, sometimes both and I would be running back to do whatever I was doing with a smile on my face. In the last few years, he's gotten more and more strict and it's mum that I now go to with any of my problems.

There's no real homework to do, just a bit of reading which neither of us are going to bother with so we have the music on low while browsing through for something to watch.

Azra has an extremely varied taste in music, and he's introduced me to stuff that I would never have even considered listening to. Some of it really good, while others are not what I would put on if he wasn't here. But then he probably thinks the same about my choices. I hear the front door close and a few seconds later mum called out.

"Honey, are you home?"

“We’re upstairs ma.” I yell back through the door.

Azra was sitting on the floor leaning back against my bed. I got on from the other side and crawl over to him, then lean over and kiss his forehead. When he looked up at me I move my kisses down over his nose, to his lips.

When we take a breath, Azra laughed. “That’s the first time I've ever kissed anyone upside down,” he said with a smile. Azra turned around and knelt beside the bed, then ran his hands through my hair before kissing me again.

“Honey, dinners ready in ten minutes,” called mum, from downstairs.

“Dammit,” I curse, jumping away from Azra and reach for my phone to check the time. It’s almost 6:45. Where the hell did all the time go. “Damn, damn, damn,” I repeat while we both rush around trying to get his stuff together and dumping it into his bag.

“C’mon,” I hiss urgently and pull him forward as we dash to the front door. With a final kiss and a hug on the porch, Azra left and I closed the door behind him.

“Honey,” called my father from the kitchen as I’m heading back to my room.

Damn!

“Yes dad,” I answer meekly, walking slowly into the kitchen. Mum was filling a plate from a pot at the cooker, and dad was sitting at the dining table. My hands are behind my back and I stare at the floor as I stood in front of him.

“What’s the time Honey?”

“6:49 dad,” I answer, without looking up.

“I thought that we had an agreement, Honey. Azra is welcome to come here, as long as he leaves by 6:30. And yet this is the second time I’ve had to speak to you about this.”

“Sorry dad.”

“That’s exactly what you said the last time,” dad sighed. “If you can't keep your end of the agreement, then we might have to rethink ours.”

My head jerked up at that. “What do you mean?” I ask slowly.

“If you can't be responsible enough to keep to a simple time, then I have to wonder if you're responsible enough to have a boyfriend,” he announced.

“No,” I gasp, taking a step forward. “I'm…I'm sorry dad, I just lost track of time. I promise it won’t happen again. I'll make sure it never happens again.”

“See that it doesn’t,” dad replied sternly.

“I know it seems harsh Honey,” said mum, putting a heaped plate in front of dad. “But rules exist for a reason, and the best way for you to show that you can handle responsibility is by following those rules.”

“Yes ma.”

“Why don’t you go wash up,” mum continued as she put another plate on the table for me.

“Yes ma,” I repeat, walking to the sink.

Troubling Thoughts

We are a couple of weeks into the term now and things couldn't be any better. I spend the bulk of my time with Azra, and I've set an alarm on my phone for 6:20 so that we can get his stuff and leave before the 6:30 deadline as I don't want to give my dad any reason to say anything.

I also make sure to put aside enough time to hang around with Carol. Azra has started to make a few friends as well so this works out quite well for both of us. I'm in history right now with Carol whispering about coming to her place after school while Mr Reece our teacher, is talking about the fall of the Roman Empire, something he says catches my attention and I block out Carol to listen to him.

"... It's one of the things that we can always rely on," he announced. "Nothing lasts forever, the romans didn't and neither did any other empire. Where there is a beginning there is always an end. Everything comes to an end eventually. Everything!"

He went on talking and I turned my attention back to Carol. The lunch bell will ring in a few minutes, and we start putting all our stuff away. When it finally does Carol and I are already heading for the door.

"Dammit," swore Carol as we're walking down the corridor. "I left one of my books behind, I put it on the floor for a minute and left it there." She turned around and walked back the way we came. "You go ahead," she called over her shoulder. "I'll catch up in a minute."

"We'll wait for you outside Azra's class," I yell out to her retreating back. There's a smile on my face and I start humming while I walk. When I look up and see Azra outside his class at the other side of the hallway my smile got wider, then froze. He's talking to a girl, a very pretty girl. Azra is facing away from me, so all I can see is a bit of his cheek over his left shoulder. He hasn't seen me yet. Suddenly the girl touched his arm then leant forward and said something. They both burst out laughing.

She chose that moment to look over Azra's shoulder and we make eye contact. The smile on her face got wider as she stared at me then she said something to him before turning and walking away in the opposite direction. Anger builds up inside me as I clench my fists and quicken my pace.

"Who's that?" I ask, coming up behind Azra.

"Oh, hey Honey," Azra smiled, turning around.

"Who was that?" I repeat.

"Tracy, she's in my maths class."

"What were you talking about?" I feel jealousy burn through me, and it takes an effort to stand still.

"She didn't understand one of the problems we were working on in class so she asked me to explain it to her." Azra replied, the smile faltering on his face.

"That doesn't seem the funniest thing to laugh about." I tell him.

"Tracy made a joke about something our teacher said… Honey… are you ok?" The smile on Azra is gone, to be replaced with a look on concern.

"Found it," announced Carol from behind us with a laugh, choosing just that moment to turn up and the tension I was feeling lessens. "Thank goodness it was still there."

"Yeah…Yeah I'm fine," I tell Azra. "Sorry…"

"Come on," Carol called walking right past us. "I'm starving."

Azra touched my arm in almost the same way that the girl did to him a few seconds ago and it's an effort not to flinch when he leant forward and kissed my cheek. I smile weakly as we head towards the cafeteria.

The rest of my lessons that afternoon drag on and I barely pay any attention to what the teacher is saying. I keep thinking of that stupid girl smiling at me. Why would she do that? What does it mean? I trust Azra, I trust him with my life and I know that he would never cheat on me. But there's this tiny little traitorous part in the back of my brain that says "what if…". These thoughts and more keep chasing themselves around my head as I stare blankly ahead of me while waiting for the final bell.

At last, it finally rang, I put the book I have on the table into my bag then head for the door. Carol is just ahead of me, and I walk faster to catch up to her.

"You still ok to come over?" She asked as we make our way to the main doors to wait for Azra.

I give her a grin and nod. "I forgot to tell Azra at lunch, but I'll let him know now." I tell Carol while watching the rush of bodies pouring out the main doors. We finally spot him come out with a couple of his friends and the three of them head straight for us.

"The guys are going to watch a football game," Azra said as he kissed me. "You wanna come or should we head back to your place?"

"You coming or what Ra?" Shouted Casey, one of Azra's new friends.

"You go ahead," I tell him. "I'm going to Carol's." He gave me a hug and another kiss before running off to catch up with them. I watch him as they walk away, one hand on the pendant hanging from my neck. Azra waved from the end of the street, then they turn a corner and are lost from sight.

"You need to stop playing with that thing or you're going to wear it down," Carol said with a cheeky grin as we walk towards her apartment.

I don't know exactly when it happened, but I've taken to holding or playing with the crystal on my necklace a lot recently, especially when I'm distracted. It's become almost a comfort thing for me. I laugh nervously and let it go.

Carol lives in a two-bed apartment with her parents and baby brother Liam. Her mum gave up her job to look after the baby and now only works a few hours in the evenings and weekends. Her dad works in a bar across town. He is actually an accountant but got made redundant when his firm closed down a few months ago. He took whatever job he could get, and the bar work keeps money coming in while he looks for another job. Carol said that he's had to start travelling around for interviews as no one around here is hiring.

"What do you think about what Mr Reece was saying earlier?" I ask her.

"You're going to have to be a bit more specific Hon," Carol replied.

"You know, about everything ending and nothing lasting forever." I explain.

"Oh yeah, that's pretty much an irrefutable fact." Carol stated. "Just look around, everything proves it. That tree there will end, this road will end, in more ways than one," she laughed at the joke. "This very city for example, it wasn't always here and in a few hundred years it will either be gone or so changed that nothing is the same. That hill there was probably a mountain at some point, and it may eventually become flat land. Yeah, everything ends, why?"

"Nothing really," I mutter softly. But my mind is on Azra and my hand is back on the crystal.

We walk into Carol's place to the smell of spaghetti bolognese cooking. Liam was in his playpen reaching up to the mobile that's slowly turning above him while making cute noises, and Carol scooped him up and made some baby sounds while playing with his lips and nose. Her mum called out a hello from the kitchen, to which we both respond while heading to her room. It's a bit of a mess, not dirty just untidy, but she seemed to know exactly where everything is. I guess it's what some people would call organised chaos.

Putting Liam on her bed, Carol synced her phone with the speakers. She usually preferred tunes with a lot of base, but has to keep the volume quite low with the baby around. This annoys her a bit but Carol's too fond of the little guy to make much of a fuss about it. I gave her a pair of headphones as a present on her last birthday and I see them on the table beside the speakers.

Liam giggled so I picked up the cute little tyke and began doing exactly what Carol did earlier with his nose. A few minutes later Carol took him back and started talking about this guy in school, he's in a year below us but does have a skateboard, which seems to provide an adequate replacement for her fascination with bikes for the moment. She's been talking about him a lot recently and she thinks that it's because she's a year above that has stopped him from asking her out.

"I've made it pretty obvious that I like him," she said. "And if he doesn't man up pretty soon, I'm going to ask him out myself."

I would never have the guts to ask a boy out and I look at her in awe. When I first saw Azra, I couldn't help but stare. Each time our eyes met I would look away embarrassed, but I was silently willing him to come over and talk to me. It became almost like a mantra in my mind, and on the day that he finally did start walking towards me I was so nervous I didn't know where to look. I stared at the floor so intently, but I could almost feel every step he took towards me. The words "don't walk past, please don't walk past" were on a continuous loop in my brain.

"Dinners ready in five minutes," came a shout from the kitchen. "Should I set an extra place?"

"Yes please mum," Carol shouted back. She knew that spag bol is one of my favourites and her mum is an excellent cook. Carol doesn't even need to ask if I want any. I head to the bathroom to wash up and she followed me after putting the baby back in his playpen.

As I head home after dinner my thoughts drift back to what Mr Reece and Carol were saying earlier. There's a frown on my face as the words "everything ends" and an image of Azra smiling that wonderful smile of his float through my mind.

"Wake up sleepy head," said mum as she opened the curtains. "I knocked a couple of times, but you weren't answering. It's getting late and you can't spend the whole day in bed."

It's Saturday morning, but anything past ten is late for mum and if I'm not up by then she'll come to encourage me up. She always knocks and calls out and she usually waits for me to answer before coming in. Neither of my parents go into my room at all when I'm not here unless it's on trash collection day.

I yawn and the sudden abundance of sunlight makes me squint. I try to think back to the dream I was having, but it's just fragments now and slipping away faster than I can focus on it. All I can recall is the feeling of unease it gives me. Over the last week I've been dwelling too much on what Mr Reese said, and I'm pretty sure that the stupid dream was about that. My hand moves to my neck, and I rub my thumb across the pendant there, its warm surface reassures me and I finally throw back the covers and get out of bed. I stretch then head to the bathroom for a shower.

Azra will be here in a couple of hours to pick me up and I'm trying to decide what to wear. I do like pink, though not to the point where it looks like I've walked through bubble-gum. But my favourite colour is purple.

It's over an hour later and I now have a pile of clothes on my bed but I'm still no closer to choosing something. I finally settle on a simple lilac dress and I'm pretty sure it's been a while since he's seen me in it, I think it might be time to go shopping again. I don't get much of an allowance and I need to save up to buy anything I want. Mum takes me shopping whenever she goes to get herself anything, and I get to pick out something for myself as well. We're not exactly well off and some months are a bit tighter than others, but all in all we do fine.

I'm just putting on my shoes when I hear the doorbell ring, and I tense up a little when I realise that my father has answered it. I hobble to my door with one shoe on to open it and then back again. Azra gave a light knock on my wall before stepping in a minute later.

“Everything ok?” I ask, walking up to him.

“Yeah, why?”

“It's nothing,” I answer, putting one hand on his chest and the other behind his head as I pull him towards me. We come up for air a few minutes later and he gives me that smile. I lean into him and rest my head on his chest. A memory of Mr Reese's words slip into my mind and I brush them away with a frown and a subconscious wave of my hand.

“Come on, Paul's waiting in the car,” Azra said, taking my hand to lead me downstairs.

Paul is Azra's father's best friend and acts as his guardian when his parents are away. Paul lost pretty much everything he had a few years back and doesn't have a job. He also helps by driving Azra's around and in any other way he can. He is really sweet and ferociously protective of Azra.

Dinner is at a little Italian place that we found by accident. Azra really likes the risotto they serve, which is what he orders and I get a spinach ravioli.

“You looking forward to the movie?” Asked Azra.

I nod quietly since my mouth is full. It's a si-fi, something that we both enjoy. “Can I try some of your risotto?”

Azra slid his plate closer to me, and a few minutes later both our plates are in the middle of the table as we help ourselves to each other's dishes. The risotto really is good.

“I’m sorry,” I apologize when I realize that I've been eating more of it than my own. Azra laughed and pushed the plate towards me.

“Finish it,” he replied with a smile.

The movie just came out yesterday, so I don’t really know anything about it, only that it's about an asteroid heading towards earth. Azra has read a few reviews and says that they are all good. The acting is supposedly spot on, and you can really connect with the characters, the special effects are supposed to be state of the art. We’re both really looking forward to it, but what’s suddenly become a more urgent matter is that I think I ate too quickly, and I feel a burp coming. How big is it going to be? Should I leave or can I disguise it with a napkin. All this took only a split second’s thought, and I decide not to take a chance. I stand but it’s already too late and there’s no disguising the huge belch. I look around for a rock to crawl under, I can feel my face turning bright red and I don’t know what to do.

Azra doesn’t laugh, he just smiled as he took my hand and asked me to sit down.

“You're embarrassed,” he said quietly.

He's still holding my hand as I sit and stare at the table, unable to look up I nod slowly, just the slightest movement of my head.

“Don’t be,” he whispered, gently squeezing my hand. “I never ever want you to be embarrassed in front of me about anything.”

He leant forward and brushed the side of my cheek with the thumb of his free hand, just the lightest of touches as he kissed the top of my forehead. Then he sat back down and waited quietly.

When I finally have the courage to look up again, Azra just has that amazing smile on his face. He didn’t let go of my hand.

It's almost 9:30 at night now and I'm sitting crossed legged on the couch at home, dad is on the big sofa watching a football game and mum is sitting beside him reading a book. There is a magazine open on my lap but I'm not even looking at it, the only thing on my mind is my date with Azra earlier. The movie really shook me up, I went in feeling on top of the world. Not so much when I came out again though. Azra really liked it, really lived up to all the hype he said, definitely worth watching. I smiled and agreed with him, the acting really was very good and that just made it even more unsettling. Azra picked up on my unease, but I think that he put it down to the incident at the restaurant earlier. He didn't pry, just held me closer.

Why the hell would they make an ending like that? Endings are supposed to be happy, the good guys win, the bad guys lose, and people walk off into the sunset. That's what a proper ending is. They're not supposed to smash an asteroid into the world and kill everyone. Mr Reese's voice echoes through my mind... "Everything ends...." And I shake my head in an effort to pry the thought loose and deny it.

Mum lets out a sigh and closed the book she'd been reading, a smile across her face.

"Enjoying it?" I ask her in an attempt to divert my attention from the direction my thoughts were going in.

"Just finished it actually," mum replied, while stretching. "It was good."

"You've been reading that book for a while now," I comment as I turn the page on my magazine. "You usually finish them a lot quicker than that."

"It was really good," mum said, emphasizing the word really and stretching it out. "I rushed through the first half, then had to make an effort to slow down to make it last." She let out a little laugh. "Oh well, you know what they say about good things."

"No," I reply, turning another page without looking at it. "What do they say?"

"All good things must come to an end."

I almost fall as I jump off the sofa, the magazine fluttering to the floor in a rustle of pages. "WHAT?? What did you say?"

"What?" Echoed mum, looking confused.

Even dad took his attention off the tv to turn to me. "What's wrong Honey?"

"That thing you just said about endings," I stammer, waving a finger at mum. "Why did you say that? What did you mean by it?"

Mum looked at dad then back to me. "It's just an expression Honey," mum explained reassuringly, getting up and walking to me. "What's the matter?" She asked, putting a hand on my shoulder.

I shake her hand off and rush up to my room, slamming the door closed behind me. "It can't be…it won't…. I won't let it…" I mutter under my breath as I pace up and down the floor. A shiver passes through me, and I stop to sit on the side of my bed. I shake my head in an effort to try and stop the thoughts I'm having, then get up and start pacing again muttering half formed sentences while still shaking my head. Jumping back onto my bed I pull the covers up to my waist as another, more violent shiver passes through me.

A thought has been forming in my head for a while now. I've managed to brush it away and ignore it every time so far. I lie down on my side and pull my knees up to my chest as it finally becomes coherent and inserts itself into my brain. If everything must end, then at some point Azra and I are going to end.

I'm shivering continuously now.

I didn't sleep well at all last night, my mind seemed to be on overdrive and my thoughts kept spinning off in directions that I didn't want them to take. Every time I felt that I was dropping off to sleep I would jerk wide awake. I don't know exactly what time I eventually fell asleep but when I last looked at my phone it was past 3am.

Azra called me this afternoon and asked if it was ok for him to come over, I told him that I wasn't feeling well and that I just needed a bit of rest. This is the first time that I've made an excuse not to see him and I'm not at all happy about that, but after my ugly little revelation last night, the thought of seeing him caused a tightness in my chest.

Monday morning, it was another uneasy night of lying awake with my thoughts running wild. I think I fell asleep earlier than the previous night but I'm not sure. I try to concentrate on what the teachers are saying but it isn't easy and my mind keeps wandering. When the lunch bell finally rang, I'm the first one out of the room. I know that Azra is usually last out of his class, and I head in that direction, but I feel a bit nervous about seeing him. When he sees me, the way his eyes light up overshadowed any nervousness I feel, and I pick up my pace.

"Hey," he smiled, giving me a hug. "How are you feeling?"

"I'm fine now," I reply. "Probably just something I ate."

"Well you did wolf down that risotto," Azra grinned and began patting my back as if he's trying to burp me.

"Stop that." I stick a finger in his ribs.

"Hey, no fair. You know how ticklish I am." Azra laughed, jumping back.

"Exactly, I know all your weak spots." I warn as I stalk him with my fingers out.

I lunge for him, but he ducked under my arms and grabbed me around the waist from behind. I burst out laughing as he lifted me up and swung me around.

When he finally put me down, I turn and rest my head on his chest. “I needed that,” I whisper to him.

It's night now, and any reassurance I felt earlier have left me as I now lie here in the dark. It’s funny how the harder you try not to think of something, the more your mind takes you right back to it. No matter how much I try to distract myself, I keep coming back to that one sentence. Azra and I are going to end.

Decisions

I reach out and turn the alarm on my phone off, I've already been awake for over an hour now. No sweet dreams for me for a while now, it's been about three weeks since my revelation and every night it's an effort to fall asleep. Each morning I wake up with a start, usually between an hour or two before my alarm. I don't remember much of the content of the nightmares I've been having, but the emotion, the fear is there in spades. I can't ever get back to sleep once I wake up, so I just lie in the dark and ruminate, my thoughts moving in directions that I don't like but have no control over. When my alarm finally rings it's a mixed blessing, I have trouble finding the energy or the motivation to get up, but neither is my bed the comforting place it used to be.

With a heavy sigh that seems to come from some bottomless pit within me I slowly push the covers back and get up, then sit on the side of my bed and stare at nothing for what feels like a few minutes but is probably longer. With another sigh I stand and head for a shower.

"Scrambled eggs, toast and a cup of tea. Breakfast of champions," said mum as she put a plate in front of me. "Better hurry, you don't want to be late".

I keep a neutral face while I slowly eat, every mouthful feels like a solid lump and it's only with a sip of tea that I'm able to force it down my throat. Halfway through I give up and push the plate away. Grabbing my bag, I make for the door.

My feet drag as I walk to school, each step feels heavy. Those damn words in my head have found a little corner inside my brain and dug themselves in, and no amount of reasoning seem to be shifting them. They feel like a sword hanging over my head, held up by a thread that threatens to snap at any moment and split me in two. I haven't spoken to Azra about any of this. How do you even bring up a subject like this? "So, Azra when are you planning to break up with me then"?

Wait, what? Where did that come from? How did us splitting up turn into him dumping me? I stop and look around, although I'm not sure what I'm expecting to see. I feel a shudder pass through me, but there's nothing out of place. Someone brushes past me in a rush to get wherever they are going, and I almost snarl a swearword at them then stop myself. I shake my head and start walking. My hand is on the pendant and the words in my head seem to have gotten a little bigger.

When I turn the last corner before the school I stop again. I give myself a little mental shake and as I count backwards from ten, then square my shoulders and stand up straight. When I reach zero, I take a deep breath and carry on walking. I don't want Azra to see how upset I am, he knows I haven't been myself. I've fended off his concerns with a smile and "I didn't sleep well," or "it's just a cold" there are a few other excuses, but I always look away when I use them.

I don't know why, but today I stand in front of the main doors and wait for the first bell to ring before I walk in the school hall.

"Hon… Hey Hon," whispered Carol as loud as she possibly could without drawing the teacher's attention.

"What?" I reply, finally turning to her.

"You ok?" she asked, a look of concern on her face.

"Yeah, yeah I'm fine," I lie, turning back to our teacher.

"I've been talking to you for the last few minutes now and you haven't heard a single word I said, have you?"

"I'm sorry Carol," I apologised. "My mind just wandered, what were you saying?" I look back at her and try to concentrate on what she's saying this time.

"It's ok. I doubt it's as important as whatever's on your mind." Carol stated. "You gonna tell me about it?"

Should I? I wonder. What exactly would I say? How would I start? I do want to tell Carol everything, but I've played the conversation we would have several times in my head and if I'm honest with myself, I come out sounding a little crazy. It's hard enough trying to get my mind around the thought of losing Azra. How would I cope with Carol starting to look at me weirdly? And even if she did accept everything I say, what exactly would she be able to do? She can't actually stop Azra from breaking up with me. And there's nothing she can possibly say to make me stop thinking about it either. Which means that there's just too much to lose and nothing to gain by telling her.

The bell rings and jolts me out of my thoughts. Carol already has all stuff in her bag, so I just dump everything inside mine and get up with her. We're almost the last to leave the classroom and I try to settle my bag while we walk towards Azra's class.

Lunch seems to be rice and some sort of mixed veg which I can't even remember selecting. After a few mouthfuls the stuff begins to taste like paper and is just as hard to swallow, I start pushing it around my plate.

"Why don't we go to the library"? Suggested Azra, looking at the fine spray of rain outside the window.

I nod vaguely and the three of us pick up our plates and dump them with the rest on our way out.

"Are you ok Honey?" Azra asked, a note of concern in his voice. "You've hardly said anything for a while."

"That's what I was saying earlier too," Carol piped in. "I had a whole conversation with her, before realising that she hadn't heard a single word I said."

"Yeah?" Remarked Azra.

"Uh huh, I might have thought she was ignoring me if I didn't know better."

"Is there anything you wanna talk about Honey?" Coaxed Azra.

“I'm fine,” I answer through gritted teeth, annoyed at hearing them talk about me.

“Are you sure?” He persisted. “You haven’t been your usual self for a while now and…”

“I said I'm fine,” I snapped. “Why can't you just leave it? … I sigh and swallow the rest of the words on the tip of my tongue.... “I’m sorry. I…I need to use the bathroom, You two go ahead and I'll meet you there,” I tell them, then turn around and head in the opposite direction. I can feel both their eyes on my back as I walk away.

I stare at my reflection in the bathroom mirror for a few minutes before opening the tap and splashing some water on my face, then use a tissue from my bag to dab myself dry. After a deep sigh and a few moments to compose myself, I walk back out again.

“I'm sorry about that,” I apologise when I join Azra and Carol in the library. “I haven’t been sleeping well these last few days and I guess it’s making me a bit irritable.”

“It’s fine.” Azra tries to give me a reassuring smile, but I still see the concern in his eyes.

I wake up with a jolt, covered in sweat and kick the blanket off me, the night air starts to cool me down and I fumble for my phone in the dark to check the time. The dreams have gotten worse these last couple of weeks, they are more vivid and I'm remembering them now. That damn sword is in them all, hanging above me like death, sometimes it's as big as a house. At times I see the whole thing, in others just the tip of it through a haze. The worst ones are where I can't bear to look up at all. It’s just an overwhelming feeling of menace hovering there above me, and I know for certain that if I do look up what I see will destroy me utterly.

Azra is going to leave me soon, I know it for a fact, just as I know that it's my own fault, but I can't seem to help myself. I've begun snapping at him for the tiniest reasons, then feel horrible about it. The lack of sleep has me continuously on edge, and even Carol tip toes around me. I think back to how I used to feel whenever I saw Azra and start crying. Now the first thing that enters my mind every morning is "will today be the day?"

I love him so much, I can't bear to be without him and I love him more every day. If he leaves me now, it's going to shatter me. I think about how much worse it's going to feel in a month or God help me even longer, how long can I go on feeling like this? This constant waiting for it to happen is like walking on the edge of a high precipice, and it's taking all my concentration to keep my balance. While also knowing that as soon as Azra breaks up with me, I'm going to fall. I'm always on edge and my nerves are frayed to almost breaking point. I can't go on like this.

If he doesn't do it soon, I think bitterly. Maybe I should.

I turn my head in disgust at that thought.

I've been staring at the ceiling for what feels like hours as I wait for the sun to rise. My alarm finally sounds, and I turn to look at the screen flashing, the vibration causing the phone to rattle against wooden top of my bedside cabinet. A second later I switch the damn thing off.

Now that I have to get up, I no longer want to, and I wonder if I can get away with skipping my shower. I remember how sweaty I was earlier and decide, probably not. After several failed attempts to get out of bed, I finally stand and trudge across to the bathroom.

There's been a battle raging within me for over a week since that thought. I don't want to break up with Azra, but it's got to be better than what I'm going through now… hasn't it? There's no way that I can feel any worse than this.

School was horrendous once again, I almost snapped at Azra a few times. I managed to hold it in, but that made me even more irritable. He asked if he could come over after school, I made up yet another excuse to stop him. I'm pretty sure that he knows I'm lying, but he hasn't confronted me on it yet.

I've been sitting on my bedroom floor for at least an hour now with my phone in front of me, I've reached for it several times but snatched my hand back each time.

I can't go on like this, I decide as I pick the phone up. When I select Azra's name, his photo comes up. I put it back down and start crying.

It's a while before I finally force myself to stop, I pick up the phone again and try not to look at him as I press call.

Azra picked up on the third ring. "We need to talk," is all I can say.

"I'll be there in ten minutes," he replied softly.

I hang up before he can say anything else. I leave the phone on the floor and walk out of the house to the sidewalk to wait for him.

When his car pulled up there was nowhere to park so Azra got out on the road. He said something to Paul who drove off, then walked towards me. Azra stopped a couple of meters away and smiled at me nervously, as if moving any closer would scare me away. The look on his face says it all, he knows it's going to be bad but he's not sure how bad. His eyes are on me the whole time.

He took a breath and said "Hey."

I feel like I'm on autopilot as soon as I start talking, like I'm looking out through the eyes of a body that I have no control over.

"I can't go out with you anymore," I say quietly. My voice is steady. Steadier than I expect, steadier than it should be.

"What? Why?" He took a step forward, then stopped when he saw me take a step back.

"Was it something I said?" He asked hurriedly. "Something I did?"

"It isn't anything you've done," I reply uncertainly. "It's me." I hear a sound inside my head as the words tumble out of me.

"What?" He repeated. "What does that even mean? We can talk about this. We can work it out. Honey... please...," Azra begged. "Don't do this."

"Please don't...," my voice finally starts to crack, and I look down. "Don't make this harder for me Azra." I realise that the sound in my head is a voice... and it's screaming.

"Make it harder for you?" Azra whispered. "Oh Honey.... how could you? You've just broken my heart into a million pieces."

Azra's standing in front of me before I even realise that he's moved, he reached for the necklace around my neck. He doesn't pull, it just came away in his hand.

"I guess you won't be wanting this anymore," he said softly as he turned and threw it.

When Azra faced me again there were tears streaming down his face. He didn't try to wipe them as he took a few steps back, then turned and ran.

I don't feel my knees hit the sidewalk as my heart splits open and my legs collapse under me. I'm having trouble breathing as I sob hysterically. That sword is no longer hanging over my head. It's sticking out of my chest now.

Someone is holding me, saying something. But I can't focus on who it is or what they are saying.

"It's ok Honey, I've got you, I'm here...JOHN GET DOWN HERE." I realise its mum, she's trying to move me, but I'm just dead weight in her hands.

I'm being lifted now, carried.

"What happened, did someone..."

“I don’t know, oh God, her knees are bleeding.”

I'm on the sofa, dads sitting on the floor in front of me. Mums leaning over, holding my face. “Honey look at me, focus on me, what happened? You need to tell me what happened.”

“It’s Azra,” I choke out. “We broke up.” My hand goes to my neck, but it’s not there…

I stand so suddenly that mum got knocked back. I head for the door, but they’re holding me, pulling me back.

“No, no, where are you going? You need to sit down.”

“It’s out there,” I shout, desperately struggling against them. “He threw it away; I need to find it.”

“What’s out there, what do you need to find?” Pleaded mum, trying to get me back on the sofa.

What’s wrong with them? Why won’t they listen? “My necklace,” I scream, fighting against my parents while trying to reach the door. “I have to get it.”

“Honey… HONEY, listen to me, it’s dark out there. You’ll never find it now. Tomorrow, tomorrow when it’s light.”

“It’s all I have left of him, “I sob, all the strength draining out of me and I collapse back onto the sofa.

Dad started bandaging my knees again, when he finished he carried me up to my room and put me on my bed. I hear the door close behind them when they leave. I crawl under the cover and pull it over my head, tears are still streaming down my face.

My alarm sounds the next morning, I turn it off then pull the cover back over my head as I curl up on my side and start crying again.

At some point there’s a knock on my door and I hear it open. I know its mum; she has a lighter knock than dad. She didn’t open the curtains this time, just walked to my bed and slowly pulled the cover down from my face.

"Do you want to talk," she asked gently while stroking my hair.

"No"

She kissed me, then walked out and closed the door behind her.

I cover my head again and reach for my necklace, only to find it missing. With a sigh I push the cover back and get out of bed. I change and leave my clothes where they fall, then leave my room, go downstairs and walk out of the house to look for my necklace.

It's dark when I come back in. I go up to my room, crawl under the cover and start crying again.

After a while mum knocked and came in again. I hear her put something down on the bedside table. "You need to eat," she said quietly. "It's Saturday tomorrow, but you'll need to go back to school on Monday." She left.

My alarm sounds the next morning, I turn it off and get out of bed, change my clothes and walk out of my room. Mum's standing there.

"Shower," she said simply.

I walk to the bathroom and brush my teeth. I finish showering then open the door. Mums standing there. A plate in one hand, a cup of tea in the other.

"Eat!" She handed me the plate then turned and walked into my room. I follow her. She put the tea on my bedside table then sat on the chair at my dressing table. I sit on the bed and look at the sandwich.

"Eat," she repeated.

I pick up the sandwich and tea. I bite. I chew. I sip. I swallow. I repeat till it's finished. As soon as I'm done, I stood up.

"Tell me," she said.

I sit back down." We broke up," I reply. The words coming out of my mouth sound dead.

"Did he say why?"

"He didn't do it, I did."

Her eyes widen at that, then narrow. "Why?"

I try to explain it to her.

"Are you going to explain it to him?"

"I can't face him ma, not after what I did. Not after the way he looked at me."

"He was angry," she stated.

"I wish he was." I reply quietly. "No ma, he looked at me like I had betrayed him…. And that's exactly what I did. I made him a promise, then I broke it, I broke his heart."

My face is in my hands and I'm sobbing again. Mum wrapped her arms around me while making soothing sounds. "It's ok," she whispered softly. "It's going to be ok."

No, it's not. Nothing is ever going to be ok again. I get up and walk past mum and out of the house to look for my necklace.

It's dark when I come in. I go to my room and sit at my dressing table. There's a fresh sandwich on it. I took a few bites before leaving the rest on the plate, then look at myself in the mirror. I see the guilt over my broken promise all over my face. Everyone is going to see it. I can feel the tears coming, I close my eyes tight and try to stop them. When I open my eyes and look in the mirror I'm scowling. I get into bed and pull the covers over my head.

Monday morning, I grab my bag and leave the house.

I come back in after mum leaves for work, drop my bag on the living room floor and go back out again to look for my necklace. It's dark when I walk in again. Another disappointing day of searching. I go straight to my room and look at myself in the mirror then close my eyes and concentrate. I open them and look at myself, not good enough. I can still see the guilt on me. I close my eyes and try again.

There's a knock on my door and mum opened it. She doesn't come in. "How was school?" She asked.

"I didn't go," I answer without looking at her.

She nodded. "I'll drive you from tomorrow," she said, closing the door. I turn back to the mirror.

It's a few hours later when mum knocked on my door again.

"Come in," I call, still staring at my mirror.

Mum walked in and closed the door behind her then goes to sit on my bed.

"Sit with me a minute, she said, patting the space beside her. "I want to talk."

"What is it?" I ask, not moving from my seat.

"Your breakup with Azra," mum replied slowly. My head snapped up and I turned to face her.

"What about it?"

I've been looking some stuff up on the net for the past couple of days and I think I found something that may explain what you went through." Mum began.

I look at her silently and wait for her to keep talking.

"It's called Anticipatory Anxiety," mum continued. "It's the fear that you feel when you think that something bad is going to happen. It's also very common, almost everyone will experience a mild form of it at some point in their life."

"If it's so common, how come I've never heard of it before?" I ask her.

"You know that feeling of fear that you have when there's a big test coming up? Or being scared when waiting to have an operation, or an important interview? That's what it is. Any upcoming event that you find scary, your mind will build up a fear around it and make you think that it's going to be huge disaster." Mum paused and looked at me then around my room.

"There's more, isn't there?" I ask her. Sensing that she hasn't told me everything.

Mum turned back to me then nodded slowly.

"Tell me."

"I'm not sure if…," she hesitated.

"There's no point only giving me half the information," I interrupt testily. "If you're going to tell me then tell me everything."

Mum nodded again, then held out her hand towards me. After a moment's hesitation I got up to take it then sat down beside her.

"Sometimes…," mum faltered then started again. "Sometimes your subconscious mind will take bits and pieces of information…, things that you see or hear. It builds up a scenario of something that may happen using this information. The fear and anxiety that you feel about this possible scenario overshadows the fact that it isn't actually a real event. Your mind…. Your fear makes you believe that it's real"

The tears are rolling down my cheeks before mum finishes. "Azra…," I sob, falling into mum's arms. "He was never going to leave me, was he?"

"I don't know for sure…," mum started, then stopped. "I'm so sorry Honey, but no. I don't think he was," she said as I wept into her shoulder.

It's Tuesday morning, I sit in mum's car and stare at the school gates for at least five minutes before I'm able to get out. Mum doesn't rush me, she waited patiently until I finally open the door and walk to the main entrance. As I stand in front of it, I close my eyes and concentrate. When I feel the mask slip over my face, I open my eyes and walk in.

The lessons drag on, I try to pay attention to what's being said but it isn't easy. My head feels like it's full of cotton and it's hard to concentrate, when the lunch bell finally rang, I breathe a sigh of relief. As I walk out of the classroom, I see Carol heading towards me. She looked at me for a second, then gave me a hug.

"You ok?" Carol asked when she let me go.

"No."

Carol nodded. "You wanna talk about it?"

"No"

She nodded again. "I've been trying to call you."

"I set my phone to reject all calls," I tell her. "What do you know?"

"Not much," Carol admitted. "He told a friend of his that the two of you broke up, nothing else."

"I need to be alone for a while," I say.

Carol hugged me again. "I'm here if you need me," she said before she walked away. I bring out my phone and take her off reject.

I avoid the cafeteria during lunch break and head towards the grounds. My feet are on autopilot and it takes me a few minutes to realise exactly where I'm going before I turn and walk in a different direction, somewhere that I can be alone. I eventually just dump my bag on the grass and slump down beside it.

God, how could I have been so stupid. What I felt before was depressing, and as bad as it was, this soul-destroying despair that surrounds me now seems to make that a walk in the park. It's like all the joy, all the light has been sucked out of me leaving just a grey shell behind.

I bring my knees up and hug them, trying to hide my face as I feel my eyes get wet. No, I won't cry. Not here, not now. But I can't stop it. It's like I'm in an unending whirlpool of desolation that's continuously dragging me deeper as I see the light above me slowly getting further and further away. And what makes everything so much worse is the fact that I'm responsible for this. I did this to us. Azra must hate me. Well, he can't hate me as much as I hate myself.

The bell to signal the end of the lunch break thankfully interrupts my train of thought, and I drag myself up while trying to wipe my eyes. I stare mindlessly at the floor while I walk back. I don't know what makes me look up, but when I do, I see Azra in the middle of the corridor. He looks up at the same time and our eyes meet, we stare at each other for a few seconds before I turn away.

No matter how fast I run I don't make it to the toilets before the tears come flooding back, I slam the door of the cubicle shut. All the pain and misery flood through me tenfold and I'm unable to stop sobbing even if I had the strength or the will to try, all I can do is ride it out.

It takes me a while before I can control myself enough to bring out my phone and look at the time, most of my lesson is over. Unlocking the cubicle door, I go over to the basin and wash my face before looking at myself in the mirror, then close my eyes and concentrate on putting the mask back on.

It's been two weeks since I saw him. I'm careful now, I check each corridor before I walk down it. Don't get me wrong, it's not that I don't want to see Azra. I just don't want him to see me. I think of him constantly, I miss him so much. I look at his photos every night as I lie in bed. Usually I think about what I would say as I beg him to forgive me. Not that I ever will. I remember the look on his face after he threw the necklace away, and it stops me every time. I still haven't found it and I've been searching every day after school.

School work is suffering… badly. I can't remember the last time I handed in any homework; I just don't care. One of my teachers even took me aside and asked if I was taking drugs. She gave me a couple of leaflets and told me to ring the number if I needed anyone to talk to.

It's almost 10 o'clock, Saturday morning and my phone is ringing. I lie in bed and try to ignore it, hoping that whoever it is will take the hint and hang up. I've been awake for a while now, but I just can't find the energy to get up. I know that I'll have to very soon, I need to go out and look for my necklace. The ringing stops, then starts again and I get an overwhelming urge to fling the damn thing against the wall when I pick it up. It's Carol. I'm tempted to reject the call, but end up answering it.

"Whatever you're doing today, cancel it. We're going out," said Carol immediately.

"I'm busy," I tell her. "Maybe some other time."

"Nope," Carol insisted stubbornly. "You've been saying that every time I call, well not anymore. I'll be there in an hour." She hung up before I could reply.

It's almost a quarter past eleven when Carol arrived and the first thing she said was…

"You're not wearing that."

"Right, let's have a look what you've got," Carol continued, then opened my closet and started rummaging through it.

"Look Carol," I begin slowly, trying not to get angry. "I'm not really in the mood to go out, there are a few things I need to do today…."

But she just ignored me while going through my clothes.

“Nope, nope, nope, maybe, nope, maybe…” After she’s been through everything in the closet, Carol looked at the maybe pile and picked out a pair of skinny black jeans and a charcoal grey top.

“Those will do,” she nodded and handed them to me.

While I changed Carol took a black coat out and threw it on the bed.

“Much better,” she smiled when I finish. “Right,” Carol grabbed my hand and pulled me to the door. “C’mon we’re going shopping.”

Shopping usually means going from shop to shop and trying on a lot of different stuff without really buying anything. There is a lot of chatting about boys, school, tv shows, the latest movies and boys. If something does catch our eye, we’ll usually spend almost an hour or more testing it on with different outfits and trying to decide if it will go well with anything we already own.

However today no matter how much Carol tried to draw me out, I just don’t engage with her. Most of my side of the conversation is a simple yes, no or I don’t know. And after the third shop she decided to stop for a coffee.

Carol ordered a Caramel Macchiato and two muffins, I'm not a coffee drinker so I get a cup of Earl Grey tea. Mum once bought it by accident, and I decided to give it a try. I didn’t know what to expect, so I was a bit tentative with that first sip. It was definitely not what I expected, but I liked it straight away. I wouldn’t have it regularly with breakfast, so I don’t really drink it at home, but I do like to indulge when we go out.

“So, you gonna tell me about it or what?” Carol asked when we found a table.

“What?” I try to deflect her question and look out of the window.

“You know exactly what I'm talking about Hon,” she persisted. “Why did you break up with Azra?”

"I don't want to talk about it," I reply, taking a sip of my tea. The citrusy flavour of the tea that I usually enjoy so much just tastes flat today.

"Come on Hon, you guys were getting on so well together. Then suddenly everything starts going downhill and you break up. What the hell happened?"

I knew this was a bad idea, and I feel the anger I've been holding in start to spill out. Why can't she just leave it alone? "Look, I told you I don't want to talk about it," I snap and stand up.

"This is for you," Carol interrupted and handed me a bag. "It's that blouse you tried on earlier. You seemed to like it, so I bought it when you weren't looking."

"I'm sorry Carol," I sigh, trying to get a hold of myself. "I know I'm not being a very good friend at the moment. I just need some time." I know it's a lie as soon as I say the words. This is one thing that time is not going to heal, but what else can I say?

Carol nodded and gave me a sad smile.

After I leave I take out the blouse to look at it. I can't remember ever seeing it before.

23rd November, 1:26pm. It's Azra's birthday today. He turned sixteen. I'm sitting on my bed with my phone in my hands looking at photos of him. I went to school this morning, but I just couldn't bear it any longer, so I walked out at the lunch break and came home. Each photo I bring up, I enlarge so that his face fills the screen while I linger on it.

There's a pile of tissues in front of me and a fresh box of them on my right. The photo I'm looking at right now is the one I use for his profile in my contacts. Azra's head is slightly bent forward, his hair falling just above his left eye and he's looking at the camera with that perfect smile. I throw another tear-filled tissue in front of me then reach for the box.

I think back to when I took the photo, it was during our lunch break and Azra was reading something to me from his phone. I set my camera to continuous shot then called out his name just as I pressed the button. There were about 30 photos in the few seconds it took for him to look up and smile at me. Most of them were blurred or just ok, but this one seemed to capture his essence in an almost perfect moment. From the way the sun reflected off his hair, to the light that danced in his eyes. And naturally that oh so wonderful smile of his that seems to have just a tiny hint of mischief in it.

I reach out to touch his face, but the phone chooses just that moment to time out, the screen turned black and Azra vanished. I'm unable to do anything but stare at the blank screen for a while. What are you doing right now Azra? Are you thinking of me? If you are, I doubt it's anything good. The phone dropped out of my hand, and I blow my nose then throw the tissue in front of me. I stare at the phone for a few moments before reaching out to pick it up. As soon as my fingers touch it, the damn thing started ringing and I snatch my hand back startled. I look at the screen and swear, its Carol.

I really do not need this right now and I go to reject the call, unfortunately my finger brush the answer button and I hear Carol start talking on the other end. With a few choice swear words under my breath, I pick it up and put it to my ear.

"…. you come over"? Asked Carol?

"No." I reply abruptly.

"Where did you go? You weren't in any of our lessons after lunch."

"I can't do this right now Carol, I'll call you later," I tell her.

"No, this can't wait. I need to see you today." Carol insisted.

I was about to hang up but the urgency in her voice causes me to bring the phone back to my ear.

"You need to come over," Carol continued urgently. "I have to go straight home after school to babysit, so if you don't come to me, I'll come to your place as soon as my mum gets back. But it will be quite late then."

"What's wrong?" I ask her. It must be serious if she's willing to come over that late. "Are you ok?"

"It's not something I can talk about over the phone, are you coming?" Carol repeated.

"Fine," I finally agree. "I'll be over later."

Carol is holding her baby brother when she opened the door to let me in. After putting him in his playpen she went to the fridge. There's a can of cola in each hand when she turned around. I take one from her and we walk to her room.

"There was an incident in class...," Carol began, then paused to open the can and take a sip. I do the same.

"Azra hasn't said a word in class since... well you know. He walks in quietly at the start of each lesson and walks back out at the end. He ignores anyone who talks to him, even the teachers. There was a test a few days ago, when he was walking out at the end the teacher stopped him. She held out his test paper and asked him if he thought this was some sort of joke. He just looked at her and walked out without a word. I saw the paper, it was blank Hon. He didn't even write his name on it."

Carol took another drink from the can before she continued. "He walked in this morning and sat down silently, the same as any other day. Remember that boy in class I call the weasel? He's thin and tall and fancies himself a bully. But he's too much of a weasel to do anything himself. He just hangs around other bullies and encourages them on. He was talking about you to his friend. Saying that now you're available, he's in with a chance." Carol paused and turned away for a second. "He said that he liked the taste of Honey and wouldn't mind a sip."

Carol stopped to look at me before she continued.

"It was like someone had flipped a switch in Azra. He stood up so quickly that his chair almost fell over."

"What…? What was that?" Azra said and turned to the weasel.

"What did you just say?" He repeated as he walked over. "Say that again," he demanded, Azra put his hands on the weasel's desk and leaned over. His voice was low but there's a hardness to it, an edge. The weasel had backed his chair all the way to the desk behind him. His head darting from side to side like he's looking for a place to run, but he's not sure where.

Mr De Silva, our teacher grabbed Azra's arm and told him to get back to his desk. To go sit down.

Azra turned to Mr De Silva and said, "Don't Touch Me," in such a tone and look on his face that Mr De Silva immediately let go and took a step back. Azra turned back to the weasel and grabbed him by the collar. "Go on say that again," he commanded.

From the sound of his voice, I knew that he was literally about to tear the weasel limb from limb, and before I knew what I'm doing I'm out of my chair and had my hand on his arm. "Let him go," I said softly. "He didn't mean anything by it, he doesn't know what he's saying."

Azra ignored me, I don't think that he even realised I was there. "Honey wouldn't want you to," I whisper so softly that I doubted he even heard me.

His head jerked to me so suddenly that I almost stepped back. I had force myself to stay where I was and keep eye contact. He blinked a couple of times before finally focusing on me. Eventually he let go of the weasel, walked back to his chair and sat down.

I watch Carol take a long sip from the can when she finished talking. I do the same.

“I asked him to the Christmas Dance,” she said suddenly, and I spray everything in my mouth over the carpet.

“WHAT?” I demand, wiping my mouth with the back of my hand and glare at her. I'm standing now.

“It’s not like that,” she insisted quickly, reaching out for the drawer beside her bed. “It’s nothing like that,” she repeated as she pulled out some tissues and held them out to me.

I stare at her without moving. “What’s it like then Carol?” I grind my teeth as I spit the words out.

Carols on her knees dabbing the spots of cola all over her carpet. “He hasn’t been here long enough to make proper friends,” she explained while moving around the carpet. “He's pushed away the guys he was hanging around with, his parents are away. He's alone, he doesn’t have anyone here.” She put the tissues in the basket beside her desk and turned to me.

“Don’t you get it Hon?” Carol persisted, taking hold of my arm. “The weasel has his trigger now, he knows how he can provoke Azra, and he's going to use it. Azra’s going to be getting into fights, a lot of fights. He's going to hurt someone or he's going to get hurt.... Badly. He's in a hole right now, I just thought that I could help pull him out. I just thought that you wouldn’t want to see him get hurt that’s all...,” she trailed off.

“He said yes?” I force the words out. I've had two boys ask me out. I turned them down, bluntly.

“What? Of course not,” she answered. “He turned me down, just like the other girl.”

“Other girl?” I ask, confused.

“He had another girl ask him out. She’s in his maths class, quite pretty, but I don’t know her name.”

Tracy, I think immediately.

“He turned her down. He was very polite about it, not a good time, he said, wouldn’t be very good company. Look Honey this isn't about romance I'm not into geeks, even the good-looking ones. I'll leave it if you tell me to."

OF COURSE I WANT YOU TO LEAVE IT, YOU STUPID BITCH!! Flashes through my head. But all that comes out of my mouth is. "Do what you want."

"You leaving already?" Carol asked, when I walk out of her room.

"I haven't been well, I think I'm coming down with something," I lie as I stride out of her apartment.

Anger builds inside me as I walk out of the building, thoughts of my hands around Carol's throat as I squeeze harder and harder. I sigh. The anger turns to jealousy, and I imagine them dancing together. His arms around her while they look into each other's eyes, as they both lean towards each other... It's anger again and I grab Carol's face in my hands and plunge my thumbs deep into her eyes. I sigh again.

Azra didn't ever take me dancing and I wonder what it would be like. His hands on my waist smiling that smile of his as we go round... tears are rolling down my face and I realise that I'm running, I keep running all the way home.

The house is still empty when I let myself in. I walk straight into the kitchen and open a drawer; I look at the selection of knives inside and wonder if physical pain would help to distract me from this living hell my life has become. I slide my hand over the knives, feeling the sharp edges scrap against my fingers. An idea comes to me, and I close the drawer.

The house is silent, almost eerily so and the air feels heavy as I walk up the stairs and into the bathroom. The mirrored cabinet on the wall is where dad keeps his razors, it's a pack of eight with five still inside and I'm confident that he won't miss one. Snapping the head off, I throw the handle into my bin, then take it back out and slip it into my backpack to dispose of outside. About ten minutes later I stare at the twisted head with its bent blades and realize I'm going to need a better plan to take it apart.

Another razor and twenty seconds with a pair of pilers and I have a couple of small blades on the bed in front of me. I put all the bits of plastic into my bag then pick up one of the shiny pieces of metal and pull up my sleeve.

I look at the little blade in my fingers then at my arm, wondering where to make the cut. Before I even realise what I'm doing I slide the sharp piece of metal against my upper forearm and pull it along my skin. The sting I feel is sharp, but not as painful as I had imagined it would be and I stare at the cut I've made. It takes a moment before the blood begins to appear, a thin red line at first that grows in little welts and I watch them get larger then stop.

I had expected more, so much more. I thought that the blood would flow, sliding down my arm in a march of red, like rain rolling down a window. The disappointment in me becomes anger and I fling the damned blade away from me, tears streaming down my face while the shadow in my stomach grew and spread.

The knock on my door is unexpected and instinct kicked in. Sliding my sleeve down and covering the remaining blade with my blanket I call out in a shaky voice. "Come in."

"How are you holding up?" Mum asked sadly as she walked in and sat on the bed.

"Fine." I lie, staring at my bedroom door and deciding that I'm going to need a lock on it.

Mum began talking but a glint on the floor draws my eye and I see the blade I threw earlier. I glance at it then turn away quickly so that I don't draw her attention to it. The sting from the cut I made didn't last and I don't even feel it anymore. I come to the realization that I'm going to have to cut deeper next time as I get off my bed and grab my coat.

"W-where are you going?" stammered mum mid-sentence.

"I need to look for my necklace," I state simply and walk out.

When I come back in later mum and dad are in the living room watching tv. Neither of them say anything when I go up to my room and close the door behind me. I don't bother to turn on the light, I just crawl into bed and get under the covers.

The nights are the worst. When I lie here in the dark, and the utter desolation of it all overtakes me. I am alone in the world. All around me is darkness and people are but shadows with nothing of meaning to say, no words of comfort that can ever reach me, all I am is just a shell, empty and hollow, that walks and talks and pretends to be alive.

Oh Azra.

Do you ever think of me?

When your mind starts to wander,

and your thoughts begin to drift.

Do my words ever echo,

In the silence of the night,

When even whispers are like ghosts,

Carried by the wind.

Am I stupid to think that you would ever take me back? I miss you so much. My heart screams for you, for your smile, your touch, your lips on mine. I know that it's foolish to hope, because even hope has deserted me. I am nothing, a fool and even my thoughts turn against me. Because no matter how much I try not to, I just keep thinking of the moment that I tore both our hearts apart.

I turn on my side and hug my knees to my chest as the tears flow freely. This is what I go through every single night.

Carol

The Christmas Dance is something the school arranges every year. It's held on a Saturday two weeks before school closes for the holidays.

Carol stood in front of the tall building and looked up. Expensive, she thinks. Not at all like the complex that she lives in. She stared at the huge glass doors with its polished brass handles for a moment before walking up the five stairs and pulling one open.

"Can I help you Miss?" Said the concierge behind the desk.

"Azra, he's on the top floor."

Just a moment Miss, I'll see if he's in, who should I say is calling?

"Carol," I reply.

The concierge spoke on the phone for a moment then looked at me, talked some more, nodded a couple of times then put the phone down. He pointed to the elevator. "Penthouse, number 1."

The doors slide open as soon as I press the button, after walking into the spacious cube I look at the list of floors before selecting Penthouse, then turn and look at myself in the huge mirror that made up the entire back wall of the elevator. I'm wearing a deep blue dress that comes to my knees along with high heels. I hate dresses and I hate heels, but I look good. I'm much earlier then what would be normal, and I managed to get on the elevator easier than I expected. I hope the rest of my plan goes as well.

When the doors open I step out and look around, I'm in the middle of a corridor stretching left and right that has seven doors. Number 4 is in front of me, five, six and seven are on my right. Number 1 is at the end of a short corridor on my left, I pass two and three on my way. I stop in front of Azra's door and take a minute before knocking. A few moments later the door opened, Azra's wearing sweatpants, a t shirt and a puzzled expression on his face.

"Hi Carol, what are you doing here?" He doesn't invite me in.

"We are supposed to go out today." I reply.

Azra looked down for a second then back at me. "You asked me out, and I said no. Remember?"

"And I told you that you didn't have a choice." I remind him.

"Go away Carol," Azra sighed and shut the door in my face.

I start smacking the door with the palm of my hand and he opened it again a minute later.

"Look Carol," Azra snapped. "I don't want a date; I don't want a girlfriend I just want to be left alone. Now get lost." He slammed the door in my face again.

I start smacking the door again, then pounding it with the side of my fist.

"Open the damn door Azra," I shout.

Number 2 opens, and a bearded guy stepped out. "Hey, what the hell do you think you're doing?" He yelled.

I stop pounding, "This isn't any of your concern furball." I start pounding again, with both hands now.

"You open this door right now Azra, I'm not going anywhere till I speak to you," I yell at the top of my voice.

"It's my concern when you're banging on that door girl," said beard, taking a couple of steps towards me. "You stop that right now."

"Touch me and I start screaming," I warn him.

"What the hell's wrong with you," snarled Azra when he finally opened the door.

"You want me to get rid of her boss?" Asked beard.

"No, I'll handle it," said Azra, before grabbing my arm and pulling me inside. "I don't know what your game is Carol, but those weren't exactly hints I was passing. I'm not interested in having a girlfriend."

"How about just a friend?" I say as I walk further in and look around. It's a nice place, very nice. I'm standing in a huge, long open plan living room. There's dining area on the left wall and a large kitchen past it. On the right wall are two doors with a giant tv in the middle of them. In front of the tv is a long glass coffee table and then a long black settee. There are two matching single seaters, one on each end of the coffee table. Behind me is a short wide corridor with the front door I just came through at the end. There's a third door on the back wall to my right. At the end of the living room are a pair of glass doors that lead to a large balcony. The place is very neat.

"What do you mean?" Azra asked slowly, his eyes narrowed as he looked at me suspiciously.

"Look," I reply. "I know that you don't want a girlfriend, I'm not interested in you that way either, you're just not my type. But I also know that you're going through a lot of crap right now and I just thought that you could use a friend."

"Oh… Well thank you for the offer, Carol. That's very kind of you, but I don't think that I'm very good friend material at the moment either."

Azra walked to the huge fridge and took out a bottle of cola, he popped the top and started drinking. He didn't bother to offer me one.

"Take a shower, get dressed and let's go to the party. It'll do you good to get out," I tell him. "Help to take your mind off other things."

"I don't think so," he replied, taking another sip from the bottle.

"I think that you've gotten a little bit too comfortable in this hole you've crawled into and I'm going to drag you out kicking and screaming if I have to. So shower… now, or I'll take you in there and shower you myself."

"I'd like to see you try."

"I'm sure you would," I reply with a smirk.

"Wha…," Azra stammered, cola spilling down his chin. "That's not what I meant. Thank you for coming Carol, but it's time for you to leave now." He put the bottle down and walked towards the door.

"I saw what you wanted to do to the weasel." I say softly.

Azra stopped midstride and turned to me with a frown. "What do you mean?" He asked carefully.

"You would have torn him apart if I hadn't stopped you."

Azra turned away and I realize I've hit a nerve there.

"What's going to happen the next time?" I press on. "What if there's no one around to stop you then? Or the time after that? How many people are going to get hurt Azra. How many people are YOU going to hurt?"

Azra thought for a moment then went over to the single seater, he sat and ran his hand through his hair. Then looked at me and did it again before sighing.

"I don't want to be your girlfriend," I repeat to try make him understand. "This isn't a date, just two friends going out and that's it."

Azra stared at me for quite a while before finally nodding. "Fine, we go out tonight and then you leave me alone."

"We'll see," I tell him.

"No, we won't, tonight and that's it."

"Let's make it interesting," I tease. "If you smile tonight then we go out again. If not, that's it."

"I won't smile," he replied adamantly.

"Then you've got nothing to lose," I tell him.

"Fine," he agreed at last, then got up and walked to the third door, which I assume must be the bathroom.

I head to the double doors and out onto the balcony, the light is fading but it's a great view from up here and you can see really far. There's the hill in the distance, our school is straight ahead and a huge billboard almost a mile to the left of it. You can't quite see it from here but a little further on is the bar my father works in.

I come back inside and open the first door of what's now my left. It's a bedroom, it doesn't look like it's being used. I close the door, go to the next one, open it and walk in. It's Azra's bedroom, there's a double bed against the opposite wall with a small cabinet beside it. On the left is a study table and on the right wall is another door, I open it. A walk-in wardrobe, typical rich kid, I think. Formal clothes on the left, casual on the right. Again, it's very neat. I look through the suits and pick out one I like, then a white shirt, finally I go through the ties and select one. There are five pairs of shoes on the floor. One pair looks slightly older than the rest, probably the most comfortable. I pick it up. I don't open any of the drawers, he can get his own underwear. After walking out I put the clothes on his bed and the shoes on the floor under them. Then I leave his bedroom, make myself comfortable on the sofa and start channel hopping on his tv.

Azra came out of the bathroom in a robe and went straight to his bedroom. When he walked back out he's wearing the suit I chose. Its charcoal grey and looks good on him, probably made to measure.

"Don't do it again," he stated simply.

"Just trying to make it easier," I tell him. "I didn't take you for a neat freak though."

"There's a maid," he replied.

"Of course there is. Rich kid." I chuckle.

Azra's face snapped to mine, and he scowled. "Don't call me that," he said quietly. "I don't like that word."

Another nerve, but I leave this one alone. I hold up my hands in surrender. "Sorry… I've never heard the name Azra before." I say to change the subject. "Where's it from?"

"It's an abbreviation of my full name," he replied. "One syllable in a name is good, two can be even better. But anymore, and it becomes too much of a mouthful. Don't you think so… Caroline?"

I ignore his question and ask one of my own. "So, what's your full name?"

"It doesn't matter," he declared with a finality that stated he had no intention of ever telling me. "I go with Azra, or just Ra if you wanna be lazy."

"Who's the beard in No2?"

"My guardian Paul."

"Why did he call you boss?" I ask him.

"His idea of a joke," replied Azra with a groan. "He helps drive me around."

"Is he going to drive us, or should I call a cab?"

"I'll ask him," said Azra. He pulled out his phone, tapped on it and put it too his ear. "Ten minutes," he announced and replaced the phone in his pocket.

"I'm going to freshen up," I tell him as I walk to the bathroom.

Five minutes later I walk out again.

"Let's go," I say and head to the front door.

The car is right in front as we exit the building. "The school," I tell beard when I climb in the back seat. Azra closed the door behind me then walked around to get in from the other side. About ten minutes later we get out in front of the school.

Azra looked around in confusion. "What are we doing here?" He asked as we stroll up to the main doors.

"It's where the party is," I reply, walking in.

"Umm, what sort of party is it?" He began hesitantly.

"The Christmas Dance," I reply, walking on. "I told you when I asked you out."

I realise Azra's not beside me; I stop and turn around.

"What is it?"

"I wasn't paying attention when you asked me out," he said as he looked around nervously.

"What's wrong?" I ask again, walking back to him.

Azra looked at the exit, then back to me, then at the floor.

"I can't dance," he said softly, staring at the floor.

"What do you mean you can't dance?"

"I just can't," he snapped. "I look ridiculous when I try. I've taken lessons and everything, but it's like I've got four feet and they're all lefts.... Look maybe we should just go back," he said turning back.

"No,no,no," I shout, grabbing hold of his hand. "Not after what it took to get you out of there. Just give me a minute to think."

Azra looked at the exit again, then at me then back at the exit. I pace for a minute.

"Right," I say. "Come on. I just need to get something from my locker, then we're leaving. I hate heels," I mutter, pulling off my shoes.

“Then why wear them?” Asked Azra.

“Why do you think?” I roll my eyes. “They look good, and they make you taller.” I stop in front of my locker and hand Azra my shoes while I open it, he took them without a word. I pull out a box, take the pair of trainers from it then put the shoes in and shove the box back in the locker.

“That’s better,” I mutter, wriggling my toes inside them. “Let’s go,” I say and walk back the way we came.

“Where are we going?” Azra inquired when we exit the school.

“This way,” I reply. There’s a large park a few minutes away and we walk towards it. I grab his hand and start jogging. Azra stumbled forward then shook me off.

“What are you doing?”

“What do you think?” I reply with a smile. “I'm running.” I grab his hand and start off again.

“It’s stupid,” he complained, pulling his hand free again.

“Of course it is,” I reply as we enter the park. “It’s stupid and childish and fun. Now come on.”

“Whatever.”

“Ohmygosh, I'm so sorry…I didn’t realise.” I say seriously as I turn and walk slowly back to him. “When’s the operation?”

“What operation?” Azra looked confused.

“The one to remove the stick up your butt,” I tell him and start laughing ... “Do you know the huge billboard on the other side?”

Azra nodded.

“Race you there,” I yell and take off. I don’t intend to stop again. I know his type, chivalrous. He’ll follow. The dress doesn’t make it easy, but the hem is wide which helps.

Azra watched Carol as she started to disappear from view, then looked back. He considered heading back the way he came for a moment before groaning and started jogging after her. This isn't so bad, he thought after a minute and started to pick up speed. The shoes are very comfortable, and the grass softened the impact of his steps.

"I'm just a poor girl lost in the woods," I shout out followed by a giggle.

It's a surprise when I see Azra pass me, I enjoy running and jog most days. I put on a burst of speed to try and keep up.

"Took your time," Azra announced when I reach the billboard.

"I let you win," I reply. "I know what boys are like about losing to girls."

"Uh huh, what are we doing here Carol?"

"This way," I say. "My dad works in a bar further up, we're going there."

"A bar? Will they let us in?"

"I'm always in and out," I tell him. "Everyone knows me there."

"Are you sure about this?" He asked hesitantly when we approach the bar. "This place looks kinda rough."

"Is poor little RaRa afraid of the big bad men?" I tease in a singsong voice. "Don't worry I'll keep you safe."

"I'm not scared, just cautious."

"Is that what they're calling it these days," I chuckle, holding the door open.

"Hey Carol," came a friendly voice from behind the counter when we go in. "Lookin' good."

"Hey Jane," I reply, walking up to the bartender.

"You're dads not here."

“I know, we just dropped in for a bite.”

“Watcha’ havin’?” Asked Jane

“Two fries, two colas and a portion of onion rings please Jane. I'll be back in a minute,” I tell Azra and head towards the ladies to freshen up after that jog. Its almost ten minutes when I come back out again, feeling much better.

Azra is at the old juke box in the corner. “You play?” I ask, pointing at the pool table.

“I know how to hold a cue,” he replied.

I roll my eyes. “I’ll break then,” I tell him as I drop a coin in and rack up the balls. I've been playing pool quite a bit since dad started working here and it turns out that I'm a natural at it.

Azra selected two cues from the wall and handed me one. A striped ball goes into the pocket on the break and I pot another four before missing the sixth. I’m going to have to hold back, the last thing I want to do is seven ball him.

I step back while Azra chalked his cue and went to the table. He walked around staring at the balls for a good minute before selecting his shot. It’s not the easy one I expected him to take. He pots five balls without any apparent effort and my frown deepened with every shot.

“You a hustler?” I ask as he lined up the sixth shot. It goes in but the cue ball lands badly. I smile as I look at the table. There are three balls near the cushion on the top left of the pool table. The white cue ball is at the bottom of the three, his spotted ball is at the top, just a couple of inches from the pocket but my stripe is in the middle of them, blocking his shot. The best he can do is touch his ball with a rebound off the opposite cushion. I smile again as he as looked at them while chalking his cue again. When he walked up to them, he stood on tip toe and held his cue vertical to the table.

He won’t, I think as he slammed the cue into the top of the white ball. I watch in dismay as it curved around my stripe, hit his spot and potted it. I'm wondering now if he didn't take the previous shot on purpose knowing he could do that. When he bent over to pot the black and win the game, I say.

"Your butt looks really good in those tight trousers."

Azra's miscue almost ripped a hole in the pool table, and I burst out laughing.

"What the hell? That's not fair, you did that on purpose," he yelled, turning to me with a scowl.

"Life's not fair, get over it," I reply while potting all the balls on the table. "What? Did you think I was going to let you win again?" I tell him as I head towards the food. "I don't want to give you an ego."

Azra grunted as he followed me.

"Where did you learn to play so well anyway?" I ask him when we sit and start picking at the fries and rings.

"At my previous school," Azra replied. "I used to go to the pool club with my friends."

"You must have gone a lot to get that good."

"Nah, not really. I just picked it up really quickly. I'm a fast learner."

"Smartest guy we've got," I grin.

"Yeah right," he muttered, "I doubt I'm the smartest guy in our year."

"Ooo, modest too," I laugh. "I'm not just talking about the year; I'm talking about the school."

"Now you're really having me on," he protested earnestly.

Someone walked into the bar, and I look up to see who it is. "Dammit," I groan.

"What's wrong?" Azra asked, turning to look behind him.

"The big guy that just walked in, his names Morello," I nod towards the newcomer. "He's been bothering me from the first time he saw me. Teasing me and asking me out, I don't know if he's serious or not, but I really hate it. I've threatened to call the cops on him, but he just laughs."

"Damn he's seen me, he's coming over. Look Azra," I hiss. "Whatever you do don't say a word, let me handle it."

"But..."

"Not a word," I hiss through clenched teeth.

I need to get rid of that idiot quickly, I grimace inwardly as I think of what else chivalrous guys like to do. Morello's big enough to tear Azra apart.

"Well, well, well, what's this," Morello grunted as he pulled up a chair and sat down with us. "You cheatin' on me girl?"

"Go away Morello," I groan.

"Don't be like that Carol, I'm just tryin' to be friendly here." Morello chuckled.

"I don't want you to be friendly, I don't want you to be anything. I just want you to leave." I snap.

"There's no need for that, why don't you and me......"

"Excuse me," interrupted Azra. "She asked you to leave, so if you wouldn't mind..."

"Shut up and mind you own business college boy," growled Morello menacingly. "You'll live longer that way."

Damn, I told him to be quiet. "Look Morello you're not wanted, probably not even by your mother. Why don't you do the world a favour and go jump off a building or something. And have a bath before you do, you smell like something I stepped in." As soon as the words come out of my mouth, I realize that I might have gone too far.

"Why you little…"

I see Morello tense and I realise that he's going to slap me, but it's too late to do anything. I stiffen instinctively.

His palm suddenly stops moving, Morello's got a confused look on his face, probably wondering why it hasn't hit me. He looked at his hand, Azra's holding his wrist. Morello tries to pull away but can't, which confuses him even more. Azra grabbed Morello's head and smashed it into the table, then spun on his foot and slammed the back of his fist into Morello's face. Morello flew back and crashed into the table behind him before slumping to the floor. He's not getting up anytime soon.

My mouth hung open as I stare wide eyed at Azra.

"Holy crap."

I look at Morello lying on the floor, then back at Azra.

"Holy crap," I repeat. "Ohmygod, that was amazing," I stutter, my lips turning up into a huge smile.

Azra looked at me like I've just said the opposite of what he was expecting.

"Come on let's get out of here," I grab his hand and pull him along. Azra dropped a note on the counter when we rush past.

"Where the hell did you learn to do that?" I ask when we walk out of the bar. I throw a couple of punches at the air, followed by a kick. "You into martial arts?" I giggle, trying that spinning punch of his and fail miserably, almost falling flat on my face in the process.

"I used to be," he replied quietly. "Not anymore."

"Why not," I grin. "You're really good, you should stick with it."

"I don't think so," Azra muttered, turning away.

“Brains, brawn and looks all in one pretty package,” I tease. “Impressive, very impressive. Anyway, it’s getting late, and I need to get back. You think your guy will be able to pick us up?”

“Yeah, I'll give him a call.”

About forty-five minutes later we’re standing at my front door.

“Bit of a dicey start, but things turned out ok,” I tell Azra with a grin. “Right, I'm going to be busy next week helping out with the baby, but we can go out again after.”

“What do you mean again?” He snapped. “This was a one-time deal.”

“You lost our bet. What, did you think that I didn’t see the smile on your face when you ran past me to the billboard?” I chuckle. “Now get lost.” And I slam the door in his face.

Honey

Honey's phone rang as she was tying her hair in a ponytail. She looked at the screen, it was Carol. Honey hesitated for a moment before picking it up and answering.

"Hi Hon, can you come over?" came Carol's voice through the earpiece.

"What is it?" I ask, getting annoyed. It's Sunday and I would rather be looking for my necklace than going to her place.

"I need to tell you about yesterday," Carol replied.

She can only mean the school dance. "I'll be right over," I tell her.

I'm confused about my feelings for Carol. Sometimes I hate her, sometimes I'm angry, sometimes I miss her. We've been through so much together for so long and she has always been such a solid presence for me. These new emotions whenever I think about her are not easy to deal with, especially with everything else that I'm going through. She's right about one thing though and I cling to that like a rock, I don't want Azra to get hurt. Ever.

I look at Carol's door for a few moments and try to calm myself before knocking.

Carol has Liam in her arms when she opened it.

"Mums at work, and he's being crying," she whispered softly, then stepped aside to let me in. "I've just got him settled."

I close the door quietly behind me and follow Carol to her room. There's a book on her chair which I move to the desk and sit down, then look around her room as she started talking.

"Azra slammed the door in my face twice, before I got him to let me in." Carol went on to give me a word for word account of what happened. I know that she's doing it to reassure me, but it still a huge thorn in my side that she spent time with him, and I can't.

"You could have told me that he couldn't dance," Carol remarked casually. The baby started crying at that moment and she stood, then began to gently rock him in her arms.

My head snapped to her at that, anger crowding out any other emotion inside me. I should be finding out these things about him, not her. I take deep breaths to try and calm myself as I listen to her continue. The fight really surprises me, I had no idea that he knew martial arts. How much more don't I know about Azra, I think sadly. How much more will I never find out.

"He's really fast Hon," Carol finished. "And strong, stronger than he looks."

I shoot to my feet so fast that Carol took a step back.

"I have to go," I tell her.

"What, already?" Carol protested. "You just got here, and we hardly spend any time together anymore. Can't you stay a bit longer?"

"I just remembered something I have to do," I explain and give her a hug. "It's really important, I'll call you soon."

I'm out of her apartment as fast as my legs can carry me, and I'm running again when I exit the building. One sentence of Carols keeps repeating itself over and over in my head.

"He's stronger than he looks."

I haven't been looking far enough for the necklace. I pick up my pace.

It doesn't take me long to get back to my street and when I do, I stop running and start walking to try and get my breath back. I don't even look at my house as I stride past and carry on up the sidewalk. When I get to the point where I usually turn back, I stop and look around. I stop here because I've always thought that there's no way the necklace could have come this far. But it might have gone further if he's stronger than he looks.

I start walking slowly as I scan the ground, my head swinging from side to side like I'm watching a tennis match. It takes a while to get to the end of the street at the speed that I'm walking. When I finally do I stop and glance around, then look back the way I came. I'm a long way from the house, it's impossible for the necklace to have come this far.

I've been looking for it for over a month now, what if it's not here, what if someone else has found it, what if I never find it? These thoughts and more run through my mind.

NO! It's here. I know it, I can feel it. And I don't care how long I have to look, I will find it. I concentrate on the right side of the sidewalk this time as I make my way back, it's the one that's away from the road. Someone walked past and gave me a wide berth; I don't look up. The neighbours have started giving me funny looks lately. Some of them look out of their windows as I've walked up and down the street staring at the floor or head swinging from side to side. Some cross the road when they see me coming, most if not all of them probably think I'm crazy. I just don't care.

I'm about ten meters away from my previous stopping point and disappointment grows with each step, I realise that I'm going to have to turn back in a few minutes and start checking on the other side when something catches my eye. I'm on my hand and knees in a flash and hold my breath as I scratch at the leaves and mud. My heart is racing when I pull it out and slowly bring my necklace up, the pendant swung gently and sparkled here and there as it caught the light. I stare at it in wonder for a while and release the breath I've been holding, then I'm back on my feet and running down the sidewalk as fast as I can.

As soon as I enter the house I go straight to the kitchen sink and hold the necklace under the tap trying to wash the mud off it. Then I dash up to my room and slam the door shut behind me. I look at the still wet necklace as I sit down at my dressing table, after searching so long for it, I can't believe that I've finally found it. I turn the pendant around in my palm, there are still tiny bits of grit on it between the links. I don't care, I'm just so relieved to have it back that for a few moments nothing else matters. A smile is on my face as I hold the ends of the chain and bring it up to my neck. Memories of Azra as he put it on me flood my mind and my hands freeze.

"There's a piece of my heart in that crystal, it's a fragile little thing so you have to be gentle with it".

"I promise I'll never break it."

My hands come down again as tears start rolling down my face. I can't wear the necklace, I don't deserve to.

I don't know how long I've been sitting there when there's a knock on the door and mum walked in. She wiped my face and held me. The tears keep flowing.

"I found it," I sob softly.

"Let me see." Mum didn't ask what I've found, she knows that I've been out searching for the necklace every day. I open my hand and show it to her.

"Here, let me put it on you," she offered, reaching for it.

"NO", I snap. Snatching my hand away.

"What's wrong?"

"I can't wear it," I stammer, my voice trembling..

"Why not?" Mum looked confused.

The words catch in my throat as I tell her what Azra said when he gave it to me.

"Oh, my poor baby," mum whispered as she hugged me again. "I've got an idea," she added, reaching for my hand and gently taking the necklace.

She knelt down beside me and started wrapping the chain around my wrist, then closed the clasp. After adjusting it and moving my hand around to make sure it wouldn't fall off, she looked up at me. "How does that feel?"

I lift my hand up to look at it, the crystal pendant hung from my wrist and I watch it sway gently for a moment then stop. The feeling of guilt is still there about wearing it, but it's not as strong as when I tried to put the necklace around my neck.

I nod slowly. "Thanks ma," I sniff and lean forward to hug her.

"There's a jewellery store a few blocks away that's open," she said. "Why don't we see if he can clean it up for you properly?"

I look at my wrist and nod, then stand and help mum back to her feet.

"Come on," she encouraged, taking my hand and leading me to the door.

The place is more a pawn shop than jewellery store, I think when I see the single glass window as we pull up. A ding sounds from the bell above the door when we open it and walk in. The shop is about thirty feet long with four elbow high display cabinets in a row on the left of us separating the place into two halves. The man on the other side of the cabinets put down the magazine he was reading and stood.

"Afternoon ladies, what can I do for you?" He smiled.

Mum unwound the chain from my wrist and put it on the glass in front of him. "Can you clean this up for us?" She inquired sliding the necklace toward him.

He picked it up and turned it around in his hands, then pulled out an eyepiece and brought the crystal to his face. I look at the displays as he inspected my necklace. The first was filled with a range of necklaces, each had a price tag neatly in the middle. The second had rings and earrings and the third had watches. The fourth was filled with a mix of everything and I notice that the prices are cheaper than the others.

The man removed his eyepiece and looked at me, then at mum. A few seconds later he reached under the counter to bring up a much bigger one. He turned the crystal around slowly as he peered at it through the larger lens. Finally, he removed the second eyepiece and rested his elbows on the glass as he looked at me again. The pendant swung slowly under a few inches of the chain that was visible, the rest was inside his fist.

"I can give you four hundred for it right now," he offered slowly.

"NO," I yell, my hand flew out and I grabbed the end sticking out of his fist. I tugged gently but he didn't let go. I don't want to pull too hard in case it snaps.

"Six hundred," he offered next.

"It's not for sale," I scream this time. "Let go dammit."

Mum grabbed his hand as well and he finally opened his fist to release the chain.

"A thousand," he called to my back as I storm out of the shop.

"What the hell was that about?" Mum stuttered in disbelief, unlocking the car and we got in. She glanced at me a couple of times after she started the engine and pulled the car out. I don't look at her as she drove, I'm busy wrapping the chain around my wrist. The anger I feel turns to rage as I check to see that it won't fall off.

"Damn him," I mutter under my breath. "He could have broken it."

"What the hell just happened?" Mum repeated. She snatched a glance at me quickly then concentrated on the road.

"Crazy," I state in disbelief. "He's crazy."

"He went up to a thousand," mum mumbled.

"So?" I shoot back, glaring at her.

"Nothing, nothing," she replied quickly. "It just surprised me, that's all. Did Azra tell you anything about the necklace when he gave it to you?"

"No," I answer flatly.

I stare straight ahead as we drive back in silence, but I see mum glancing at me a few times out of the corner of my eye.

Mary watched her daughter run up the stairs and slam the door of her bedroom behind her. John was on the sofa watching a football game with a beer in his hand. He looked up at the door when it slammed, then turned back to the game.

"Can we talk for a minute?" Mary asked, sitting beside her husband,

"Yeah, sure," John answered, turning the volume on the tv down.

"I think it may be important," Mary added.

John reached for the remote again and turned the tv off then replaced it back on the table. "What's wrong?" He inquired, reaching out and gently squeezing his wife's arm.

"Honey found her necklace," Mary began quietly.

"That's a good thing, isn't it?"

"I don't know, I thought so at first but now I'm not so sure," Mary admitted.

"Why not? What is it?"

Mary took a deep breath. "You love me don't you John?"

"Of course, I do. With all my heart," John assured her.

"Now how would you feel if I asked you for a divorce?"

"Angry, hurt, confused," John replied.

"And after the divorce," Mary continued. "How would you feel if I wanted to get back together? Would you want to?"

"Maybe, I don't know… it depends. Where are you going with this Mary?"

"Now imagine that we're both 16 and I've broken your heart, without even telling why. Would you still want to be with me if I asked you out again?" Mary finished.

John considered it for a minute. "No…. probably not," he finally admitted.

"Even if Honey does decide to try and get back with Azra, I doubt very much that he would want to." Mary concluded. "And now that she's found the necklace, something physical that he gave her, it's going to be even harder for her to let him go. The guilt she feels about what she did is eating her up, and I wonder if there will be anything left of my girl in the end."

"What do you think we should do?" John asked his wife softly as he reached out and hugged her.

"What can we do?" Mary wondered quietly. "Comfort her, encourage her, wipe away her tears. No more than we have been doing, at least for now."

"What do you mean, for now?"

"I'm considering maybe therapy," Mary admitted slowly.

"Really?" Gasped John. "Are you sure that's necessary?"

"I don't know," Mary sighed. "I'm not sure about anything at the moment, and I hope I'm wrong, but I think that Honey may be suffering from depression. She's on a downward spiral right now and if she can't pull herself out of it, then we may need all the help we can get. I don't think we're at that point yet, but we'll have to keep an eye on her. The longer we leave it, the harder it will be to help pull her out of it. And her having the necklace probably won't help."

"At least she won't be walking up and down the street looking for the damn thing anymore." John muttered.

"There is that," Mary agreed. "He offered her a thousand for it."

"WHAT?" John stiffened. "A thousand…"

"I think it may be worth about two or three times that," Mary stated.

"No way," john stammered. "You really think so?"

"I don't know, maybe. It was just a tiny, hole in the wall pawn shop." Mary admitted. "I'll ask her for it tomorrow and see if I can get it properly valued."

"Honey, breakfast is… oh there you are," mum smiled when she saw me walking down the stairs. "Listen, I was thinking about yesterday. We didn't even get around to cleaning your necklace after that idiot went mental on us. There's a proper jeweller on my way to work, why don't you let me have it for the day and I'll get it cleaned for you."

"You know ma, its fine. I think I'll just leave it."

"Don't be silly," mum persisted. "It's got grains of grit between the links and on the crystal. You don't want it to get damaged, do you?"

"I'll give it another wash later," I reply. The incident yesterday really shook me up, what if it broke? Passes through my mind again, or if he had refused to let go? I just found the necklace and I don't want to let it out of my sight again.

"Honey, come sit down a minute." Mum asked gently. She looked at my face and whispered. "Don't you trust me?"

"Of course, I do," I stammer. "It's just that I don't want to.... Maybe I should come with you."

"You've got school today. Look, I promise not to lose it, and I promise to put it straight back in your hands when I see you this evening".

I stare at my plate for a few minutes trying to think of some way to refuse to give it to her, but nothing comes to mind. "Ok ma," I finally agree reluctantly. I take a long look at the necklace around my wrist before taking it off and handing it to her. "Please be careful with it."

The jeweller is actually a few minutes' drive past where Mary worked. She stood in front of the large glass doors for a second before walking in.

"Good morning madam, would you like any help?" Came a voice from the other side of the store.

"Hello," replied Mary, walking up to the elderly gentleman. "I was wondering if you could clean this for me and give me a valuation on it." She took out the necklace and held it in front of him.

"Of course, why don't I clean it first," the man offered as he reached for the necklace. "Then we can have a good look at it. It will take about an hour or so, would you like to come back later?"

"I'll wait," Mary insisted as she walked over to one of the leather armchairs and sat down.

After a few minutes she opened her handbag, took out her phone and selected office from her list of contacts. "I'll be about two hours late in this morning," she said into the phone.... "No nothing major, just some family stuff.... ok, thanks, I'll see you then."

Slipping the phone back into her handbag Mary looked around the store. There were two large circular display cases directly in line with the entrance, one in front of the other. Three smaller display cases were against the left wall and another three against the right. Past these are two leather armchairs on each side of the wall and finally a long row of displays near the end wall. There was a single door on the end wall behind the displays. The whole room is painted a brilliant white and a large crystal chandelier hung from the ceiling in the centre.

It was almost an hour and a half before the man returned from behind the door and announced, “All done.”

“Well,” said the man as he lay the now gleaming necklace before Mary. “The chain is platinum obviously, very good craftsmanship. Worth about two and a half to three thousand I would hazard. The jewel however is a bit of a mystery to me, I've never seen its kind before, and I’d thought that I had seen it all.”

“It’s rare then”, stammered Mary.

“Oh yes,” confirmed the man confidently. “Very rare.”

“Expensive?” Enquired Mary, starting to feel a bit queasy.

“Definitely,” he agreed. “Though difficult to put a price on. A collector could offer you ten or fifteen thousand maybe more, however if you get two or more collectors bidding on it….” The man paused as he considered it for a second. “Well, there no telling how high they could go.”

“May I have a glass of water please,” Mary gulped unsteadily. “I don’t feel so good.”

All my focus is on the front door, as I wait for it to open. The tv is on, but I have no idea what’s showing, nor do I care. As soon as I hear the handle move, I tense and when mum walked in, I jumped up.

“Where is it ma? You’ve still got it haven’t you?” I yell, rushing up to her.

“Yes, yes I've got it, just give me a minute.” She walked into the kitchen took out a glass and a bottle of whiskey from the cabinet. After pouring herself some and downing it in a gulp she winced and then poured herself another.

“What’s going on ma? Where’s my necklace?” I ask again, getting more agitated by the second.

“We need to talk Honey,” mum replied. She carried the glass of whiskey back to the living room and stood there looking lost, as if unsure of what to do next.

“Sure ma, just give me the necklace. Then we can talk about anything you want. You promised that you would give it to me as soon as you walked in,” I remind her.

“Yes, yes I did,” she admitted, taking the necklace out of her handbag and handing it to me.

“I don’t think you should do that,” mum said when I start to wind the chain around my wrist. She took a large sip from the glass and coughed.

“Why not? And why are you drinking? You never drink when you come home from work.”

Mum finished the whiskey and sighed as she put the glass down. “It’s expensive, she said finally. Very expensive.” She explained what happened at the jewellers. “Maybe you should consider selling it,” she suggested carefully after she finished.

“WHAT? NO!!” I shout, jumping up. “I don’t care if it’s worth a penny, a thousand or a million. I don’t care if it’s worth all the money in the world. I'm never going to sell it. Never!” And I storm off to my room.

It's three days before Christmas. The school has closed for the holidays, and we have the next two weeks off. Carol called earlier, she went out with Azra again yesterday and needed to tell me about it. She’s in my room right now and has been pacing for the last couple of minutes before finally sitting down at my dressing table.

“We went for a movie and then stopped off at a burger place for a bite after,” Carol eventually began.

I'm on my bed as I stare at her, my hands are in my lap and I'm twirling the pendant between my thumb and forefinger.

“It was strange being with him,” Carol continued. “Most boys are normally only after one thing, and they are either trying to impress you or look impressive. Usually you can use that to, you know…” Carol shrugged, trying to find the right words. “Manipulate them a bit. It put me off guard that he didn't try to do any of that.” Carol bit her lip as she looked around.

“….. I kissed him,” she blurted out a second later.

Carol's words take me off guard and for a moment I just stare at her, then I'm off the bed and out of the room, just about making it to the toilet before I throw up.

“Hon I'm sorry, it was just on the cheek. I'm sorry.” Carol called through the bathroom door.

“Get out,” I shriek at the door. “GET OUT!!”

“I'm sorry Hon, it was a stupid mistake. He just froze and walked off. Honey please…”

“Get out, or so help me I'll…,” I don't get to finish my sentence before I puke again.

Mum and dad went to bed about an hour ago, they should be asleep by now so I finally slide out of bed and quietly slip downstairs into the kitchen. I stare at the drawer as I approach and gently pull it open. After checking all the knives, I finally decide on one with quite a thin blade, it seems to be the sharpest.

I'm back on my bed with only the nightlamp on as I glare at the knife laying in front of me. The low light of the lamp just about reaches the opposite wall, and the entire room is surrounded in shades of grey shadows that almost seem to grow and shrink around me. Once again, I glance at the door and wish I'd put a lock on it as I slowly reach out towards the wooden handle of the knife. Looking at the thin healed scar of my previous cut, I bring the knife up to it and tense my forearm. A moment's hesitation before I put the blade against my arm and pull it against my skin. The blood flows immediately and I'm grateful for the paper towels on my lap.

The pain is intense, so much more intense than before and I clench my jaws together as a low moan grows in my throat. I can feel my skin tear apart as the knife rips through the resistance of my flesh and I let it out a loud gasp, unable to take the pain anymore. The flow of blood isn't disappointing this time and I gape at it worriedly. I avoided all the veins that were visible, but what if I'd cut one that I couldn't see? Snatching up a handful of paper towels, I wipe my arm then hold them against the cut. I have to do this several times before the bleeding finally stops and I reach for the plasters I'd stashed in my drawer earlier.

Looking at the mess around me, I'm amazed at the number of blood-soaked towels on the bed. Gathering them up, I shove them into a plastic bag and dump the lot into my bag. There are small splashes of blood on my bed, but I'm not to worried about them. I have an easy excuse for that.

Once everything is cleared away, I gaze at my bedroom ceiling blankly while thinking about what I just did. I don't know exactly what I was expecting to happen, but I feel it should have been more than that. My arm hurts, but it doesn't diminish any of the pain I feel regarding Azra. Sure, it gave me something else to concentrate on, and the pain while I was actually cutting myself did blot everything else out, but it didn't stop me thinking about him for very long. I smile miserably at the thought of cutting myself every time I think about Azra, I'd bleed out before the day was halfway through. Turning on my side I hiss in pain after resting on my hurt arm and begin swearing angrily while trying to get into a comfortable position. Once again, I wonder if I'm missing something here.

I wake up and reach for my phone to check the time, it's 8:05, Christmas day. I bring my wrist up and look at my pendant for a moment, then lower down to the one and a half inch red scar below it, and grimace. There's a bunch of large plasters in my drawer, and I take one out to cover the cut.

Finding the necklace has turned out to be a mixed blessing. All the drive I had when I was looking for it has gone now that I have it back. I've got nothing to focus on anymore, not that I regret finding it. Even the thought of being parted from it makes me shiver. I rub the crystal with my thumb as my mind drifts back to last Christmas.

Mum always tried to make sure that she got everything a few days before Christmas Eve, but there's usually something that she's forgotten or run out of. All three of us then drove down to the store and tried to grab whatever we could among the horde of other last-minute shoppers. The few items on the list ended up being half a trolly full of stuff by the time we get to the checkout, a lot of it being snacks and junk food. When we got back, we all gorged on the snacks while watching movies. I choose the first one then mum next and lastly dad. Finally, we put all the gifts that we had bought under the tree to open the next day.

None of that this year, I think sadly. I get out of bed and go for a shower.

I can smell the bacon even before I walk down the stairs, and my stomach rumbles despite the fact that I'm not hungry. Mum put a plate of bacon, eggs and some toast in front of me when I sit. I barely manage a few mouthfuls of each before I push the plate away.

"You've hardly had any," dad coaxed. "Why don't you have a bit more?"

"I'm not hungry," I reply while staring at the table blankly.

"Come on Honey, its Christmas day. You can at least try to make an effort."

"I don't want to try, and I don't want to make an effort," I scream, before running back to my room sobbing.

Courage

It's been about a month now since Carols visit, and I've been avoiding her at school as well. She's tried to call, but I've put her back on reject. She's even started to call the landline in the last few days, sometimes twice a day. I've told mum to tell her that I'm not interested in talking when she calls.

I'm sitting on my bed staring at the pendant. I've loosened the chain so that it hung a few inches from my wrist. The crystal swung from side to side and I watch the light glinting off the facets as it slowly came to stop. I tapped it gently with my finger to start it swinging again. Mum knocked on my door, but I ignore it and keep toying with the pendant. She knocked again and I ask her to come in.

It's Carol.

I'm so surprised to see her that it takes me a few seconds to respond. "What the hell are you doing here?" I demand.

"We need to talk," Carol replied, walking into the room.

"We've got nothing to talk about, get out."

"Why did you break up with Azra?" She asked.

"That's none of your damn business, now get out or I'll throw you out," I snarl as I jump off the bed and stalk up to her.

"We're moving out," she whispered.

I stop midstride. "What do you mean?"

"Dad found another job, it's not in this city. We're leaving next week."

"Oh!" It's all I can think to say.

"We can't leave it like this Hon, this could be our last chance to talk, and we've always told each other everything. What happened to you?" She pleaded.

I walk back to the bed and sat down. She's right about one thing, we have told each other everything. We've laughed, joked and comforted each other through all our mistakes. We've always been there for each other. So why haven't I told her about this?

Because I'm ashamed to. No matter how angry I am with her, she's still my best friend. No matter how much I don't want to talk to her now, the thought of never talking to Carol again didn't enter my mind. I look around while trying to decide what to do. She's right though we can't leave it like this. I stare at Carol for a few minutes as she stood there quietly, then begin talking.

I'm sobbing again when I finish and I expect her to run up and hug me any moment now, I could really use it. Instead, she just says one word.

"Coward."

It cuts through me sharper than any knife.

"What?"

"You heard me," Carol continued. You're a coward."

"No," I gasp, unable to accept what she's saying.

"Yes, you are. You're a coward for breaking up with him, and you're a coward for not speaking to him again. Just because something must end, it doesn't mean that you have to give up on it. The less time you have, the tighter you hold on, and the more you try to squeeze out of it. You don't just walk out."

Carol marched up to me.

"No matter how much I tried, you wouldn't open up to me," she said accusingly. "How could I help if you refused to tell me anything? That's one of the reasons I asked Azra out. I hoped that he would tell me what you didn't, why exactly the two of you broke up. He refused to talk about it of course, and I always thought that it was because it was too painful. But it's not just that, is it? He doesn't even know why you did it. You didn't ever bother tell him why."

I shake my head.

"You need to tell him." She stated.

"He'll never forgive me," I sob.

"No, he probably won't," Carol acknowledged. "But it's not just about that anymore. You say that you love him, but you couldn't have hurt him any more than you did if you'd hated him. Don't be a coward for the rest of your life. Tell him Hon, he should at least know why you broke his heart." She stared at me for a few seconds before walking out.

I'm crying even harder now, because she's right. I am a coward.

It takes me a while to finally stop the tears, but the first thing I do after I have, is pick up my phone and select Azra's name. I don't hesitate and my hand doesn't shake this time when I press call.

"Can I see you?" I say into the phone when he answered. "There's some things I need to tell you."

"Should I come over?" Azra asked.

"No. I'll come to you," I reply. "I'm leaving now, I'll be there as soon as I can." I walk out of my room as soon as I hang up.

As I stand in front of his building and look at the glass doors I shiver slightly. The determination I felt earlier seems to have fled and it's all I can do not to turn around and run.

"Coward," whispered Carol in the back of my mind. I march up the stairs and walk in, the concierge seems to be expecting me because he just nods towards the elevator as soon as he saw me.

I remove the necklace from my wrist as I go up. I need to feel it's reassuring weight in the palm of my hand when I speak to Azra, and I can't do that with it wrapped around my wrist. I know exactly what I'm going to say to him, I've gone through this a hundred times or more in my head during the last few months.

I look at the number 1 on his door, then back to the elevator for a moment, then try and muster whatever courage I can before knocking.

When Azra opens the door, I just stare at him. He's wearing jeans, a black V neck t shirt and is barefoot.

"Hi," is all he says as he opened the door wider.

It takes me a few seconds before I'm able to walk in.

"Hi," I return as he closed the door behind me. I look around and try to decide where to go, then choose the dining table and walk towards it. My step falters when I suddenly realise that my mind's gone blank, and I feel an overwhelming urge to bolt for the door as I turn to look at it.

"Coward," Carol whispered in my head again.

I pull out a chair and sit, Azra chose the one opposite me. He doesn't stare at me or say anything as I try to find some words.

"There are some things I need to tell you," I begin. "I'll probably mess this up, I might repeat myself or have to start again, but I hope that you'll bear with me."

Azra looked at me and nodded.

"I didn't tell you why we.... Why I broke up with you."

"No," he replied. "I've thought about it.... A lot. I wondered if it was something I said or did, and I've tried to go through all the conversations that we've had. I then thought that there might be someone else, but you didn't start seeing anyone." Azra looked down. "Eventually I figured that you just didn't want to be with me anymore."

"NO," I burst out. "It was never you or anything you did. I'm the one who messed up, I'm the one who...." I stop and try to gather my thoughts, then look at Azra and start talking. Once the words start, they just continue flowing out of me. I tell him everything, every thought and fear. Things that I didn't tell my mother or Carol, I leave nothing out.

"I didn't ever want to leave you," I finish. "At the end I tried to stop myself, but I couldn't. It's like when you start running down a steep hill, gravity takes over and keeps pulling you forward. I was screaming at myself to stop, I just couldn't." I glance at Azra, then stare at my hands on the table. It's such a struggle to keep talking while holding back the tears that I feel building up, but I have to try.

"I wanted to run after you when you left," I say without looking up. "I curse myself that I didn't. I made a promise to you and then I broke it, I broke both our hearts that night and I've been crying ever since."

"I've seen you at school," Azra said after a pause. "You didn't look like you regretted your decision. I wanted to come and talk to you about it, but the look on your face stopped me every time."

"It was a mask," I explain hesitantly. "A mask I put on to try and hide the shame I felt. The number of times that I would run to the toilets or an empty classroom and cry my eyes out, until I could control myself long enough to put the mask back on." I shook my head. "If you had come to me, I would have grabbed onto you with both hands and not let go."

I pause for a moment and look around the room. This is the part I want to say the most while also being the one I'm terrified of.

"I messed up Azra, in the worst way possible. I know that I don't deserve to be with you, and I would understand if you said no. But I have to ask.... Do you think that there is any possibility that you would give me another chance?" I plead desperately, as I open my hand and show him the necklace.

Azra reached out as if to touch it, then stopped. "Where did you get it? I threw it away."

“I went looking for it the next day,” I reply. “It took me over a month to find it.”

Azra got up and went across to the fridge, after taking out two bottles of water he came back and slid one over to me. I leave the necklace on the table between us as we open our bottles and drink. Azra stared at it for a long moment before he started talking.

“When I left that night, I ran for as long as I could,” he began quietly. “And when I couldn’t run any more, I walked. I didn’t know where I was going, and I didn’t care. I walked for hours, the whole night in fact. Eventually, the sun started to rise, and I stopped to look at it.”

Azra took a sip of water before he continued. “It was beautiful, the most beautiful sunrise I had ever seen.... And I hated it, I screamed at it. I wished that I could reach out and tear that damned sun right out of the sky so that I could crush it in my hands, knowing that it would consume me, in fact I wanted it to, just so that it would end this pain.” Azra shook his head. “How could there still be beauty in the world,” he snarled. “How could there still be light? Didn’t anyone know what has happened? Didn’t anyone care?”

The guilt I feel at the bitterness in his voice twists my insides, and I'm unable to hold back the tears anymore, because I know that I'm responsible for his pain.

“I made my way back home eventually,” he continued softly. “It’s a good thing no one got in my way that morning, I don’t know what I would have done to them if they did. Every morning after that I would force myself out of bed, because the alternative would be to lie there and think about you, about us. And I would drag myself through each empty dead day. And as bad as the days were, the nights… the nights,” he shuddered.

“…were a thousand times worse,” I finish.

“Yes,” he whispered as he wiped his tears with the back of his hand. “A thousand times worse, only to repeat it again every morning, day after day. An endless cycle of pain stretching ahead, with no end in sight."

It took all my willpower not to get up and try to comfort him right there.

"I can't go through it again Honey. It terrifies me, it would kill me. I would rather lie down and die right now than go through that night again."

I was expecting Azra to refuse, but to actually hear it is more than I can bear. It's like a chasm has opened up at my feet, and the world around me spins as I fall in. If I wasn't already sitting down, I think I would have probably collapsed, and I grip the seat of my chair with both hands to try to anchor myself to reality. "I understand," I choke the words out before reaching out to pick up the necklace, I try to keep my balance while slowly walking towards the door. "I'm…I'm so sorry Azra."

"Where are you going?" He called to my back.

"I…. I don't know…."

"Give me the necklace."

"What?" I gasp, unable to comprehend his words for a second.

"The necklace Honey. Give it to me." Azra repeated and held out his hand.

"Oh." I look at the necklace, then at him before forcing my feet to walk back. Each step feels like a death sentence that brings me closer to oblivion. I lift my hand up and watch as my necklace slowly spills out of my palm and into his.

When his fingers close around it, I realise that I should leave, but my legs no longer seem to work.

"Turn around," Azra said softly.

"What?"

"Turn around," he repeated. "It's easier to put it on you from behind."

"What? But you said… I thought you...??" I stammer uncomprehendingly.

"I am," Azra replied slowly. "I'm terrified. But I won't let fear make my choices for me Honey. I won't let it choose what I do. I need you to promise me something if we're going to do this," he added, closing the clasp behind my neck.

"Anything," I sigh, turning around.

Azra looked into my eyes and rubbed the back of his fingers across my cheek. "Everyone has times when they doubt or get scared. There's nothing wrong with that, it's normal. Giving up when those times come, is another matter. Promise me that you won't just give in to your fears again, talk to me, tell me what you're going through and we'll work it out together."

"I promise," I reply.

He took my hands in his and looked at them, then said…

"Your hands, they're so small,

Yet within them you could hold,

My entire world."

"And I promise I will never do anything to hurt you again." I burst out as I grab him and crush him against me. His arms are around me; I feel him squeeze and for the first time in what seems like an eternity I feel something other than despair.

"I love you Azra," I whisper breathlessly.

"I love you more," he whispered back.

As I stand there holding him it feels like coming home after being lost, and I don't ever want to let go. I feel him run his fingers through my hair. Then he brought his hand down my face and gently lifted my chin up, I close my eyes and melt into his arms as our lips touch.

After what seems like too short a time Azra released me and led me to the sofa, as we lay there I rest my head on his chest and we snuggled up to each other. He starts playing with my hair again and I bring his hand up to my lips. I kiss each of his fingers and then his palm before putting it under my cheek. I drink in the sight of him, the touch of him, the smell of him. I want to etch this moment into my soul forever.

Finally Azra said, "We should go out tonight to celebrate."

"I'd like that." I reply. "Is it ok if I have some time to get ready?"

"It's coming up to twelve now," he said after glancing at the clock on the wall. "What time should I pick you up?"

"How about six?" I say against his chest.

It's more than an hour before either of us actually move, and even then, we do so reluctantly. Azra called Paul a few minutes earlier and he'll probably be waiting for us by now. When Azra goes to get a pair of trainers, I play with my pendant. I feel complete, having it around my neck again.

As soon as the doors on the elevator closed behind us, we're back in each other's arms. After a few minutes I hear a sound but put it out of my mind immediately. There's that sound again, and this time it's louder. We break off our kiss and look around, the door of the elevator is open, and the concierge is discretely clearing his throat against his hand. I don't even feel the least bit embarrassed as we walk out of the building.

Azra has one arm around my shoulders, and I hold his other hand in my lap as I lean against him, I play with his fingers and trace the lines on his palm on the drive back. When we arrive at my place, I'm reluctant to leave, but with a final hug I opened the door and stepped onto the sidewalk. I watch the car drive away down my street, until it finally turned the corner and disappeared.

Barely able to contain the excitement inside me, I run up to my front door, and it erupts in a scream as soon as I'm inside. Mum came running out of the kitchen and dad jumped off the sofa as I ran to him and threw my arms around his neck. "He said yes," I repeat over and over again. Mum's next and I run into her open arms to hug her.

"He's picking me up at six," I tell mum when I release her. "I need a new dress. I don't have enough money ma, but if you can buy it for me, you'll never have to give me an allowance ever again," I beg her.

"Don't be silly, of course we will," mum grinned. "And we should get your hair done, and maybe a little make over as well. Come on," she laughed grabbing her bag and coat. "Let's go shopping."

Azra

It's five minutes to six when we pull up to Honey's place that evening and I'm nervous as hell. I look at the flowers and chocolates in my hands, I couldn't decide which to get so I brought both. Or is both too much I think yet again as I stand on the sidewalk and look at her house. A glance back to Paul and he urged me on with a smile and a wave of his hand. After a few moments, I walked up to the door and pressed the bell.

"Hello sir," I smile at her father when he opened the door and invited me in. Her mother is standing in the living room with a huge smile, and I greet her with an "Evening ma'am," as I walk in. Honey's mum stepped to one side and my jaw dropped open.

"Oh my god…, I always knew… I mean I…but I never…" I stutter incoherently when I see Honey step out from behind her mum. "You look stunning."

It's all I can think of to say as I walk up to her.

"These are for you." I gulp, holding up the flowers and an empty hand…. "Huh?" I think, looking at my hand. I'm sure I had the chocolates when I walked in. I turn around and see her dad picking them off the floor.

"Thanks," I sheepishly take them from him and give them to Honey.

"Let me put those in some water," her mum offered, taking the flowers and going into the kitchen.

"Shall we go?" Honey smiled as she took my hand and led me to the door.

With a final look at her parents, Honey closed the door behind her.

"Hi Paul," she waved as we walked arm in arm towards the car.

"Hey Honey," Paul grinned from behind the wheel.

"So, where are we going?" Honey enquired when I opened the car door for her.

"Well, we could try out the new sushi bar that just opened," I begin as I get in behind her. "Or that little Italian place, or…"

"The Italian place," Honey interrupted. "Let's go there. It's been a bit of a favourite since…. well, you know…"

"I know," I say with a smile and touch her hair. "You look beautiful," I whisper, sliding closer.

Honey smiled and touched my cheek, then slipped her hand around my neck and pulled me towards her.

"We're here," Paul called, much too soon.

"You're covered in lipstick," Honey giggled when we separate. "Don't worry," she continued, before taking out a pack of wet wipes from her handbag. "I came prepared…. There, much better," she announced after wiping my face. "Did I miss any on me?" She asked.

"Just a tiny spot here," I tell her, taking the wipe and cleaning the smudge.

"Well, the lipstick certainly didn't last as long as I thought it would," Honey laughed when we enter the restaurant.

"Sorry," I apologise with a sheepish grin.

"Don't be silly, I was expecting it to go, which is why I brought these." She waved the wipes in the air. "Look our old table is free, let's sit there."

"I'm glad to see that back where it belongs," I tell Honey after we take our seats and order, I reach over and touch the necklace. Her hand instantly went to her neck, and she took the pendant in her hand.

"Since you've brought it up, I've been meaning to ask. Why didn't you tell me it was so expensive? I thought it was silver, not platinum and what exactly is the crystal?"

"Well…" I begin, "As to why I didn't tell you how much it costs. I wanted you to wear it, without having to worry. I knew that if I told you what it was worth, you would always think twice before wearing it. I didn't want you to do that. To be honest I hoped that sometime in the future I would tell you all about it and we could have had a good laugh."

"You think about us doing stuff in the future?" Honey whispered, wide eyed.

"Yeah," I turn away embarrassed.

"Oh Azra, I put us both through hell these past few months, I really messed up… I'm so sorry…"

"You're right, we did go through hell. But the darkest days are over now and while we won't ever forget them, there's no reason for us to dwell on it right now."

"The darkest days," Honey repeated slowly…. "Yes… yes they were."

I reached out to take her hand and gave it a gentle squeeze, after a moment I feel her squeeze back. When she looked at me, I see that Honey's eyes are brighter and to distract her from the tears that I realise are about to come, I start talking again.

"About your pendant, I don't really know what it is," I began. "I found it in a flea market, there was an old guy that was selling a whole lot of trinkets in a display box that he had on a collapsible stand. I stopped to have a look and the crystal caught my eye immediately."

Honey nodded. "How much did he want for it?"

"Well, that's the funny thing," I continue. "When I asked him about it, he seemed confused that it was in there. He told me that it wasn't for sale and that he must have put it in the case by mistake. He immediately took it out and slipped it into his coat pocket. But I wasn't about to let it go that easily and started badgering him about it."

"He didn't want to sell it?" Honey asked when our food arrived, strangely enough it's exactly the same meal that we had the last time we were here. I didn't realise that when we were ordering it.

"No," I shook my head with a mouthful of risotto. "No matter how much I pestered him, no matter how many times I raised my offer. He point blank refused to sell it. Eventually he got so annoyed that he practically screamed at me, "What the hell do you want it for so badly?"

"What did you tell him?" Honey asked while picking at her ravioli.

"The truth," I reply. "I tried everything else, and it didn't work. I told him I wanted it for you. I told him about us, about how special you were. I said that as soon as I saw the crystal, I knew that I wanted you to have it. He seemed quite taken aback by that, and for the first time I got something out of him other than a flat no."

"What did he say?" Honey enquired. She had gotten quite engrossed in the story, and I seem to have been successful in diverting her attention away from how upset she was getting earlier.

"He asked about us," I continued. "It was nothing inappropriate, just stuff like how I felt about you, how long we'd been together. He still refused to sell the crystal though. Luckily, my bank was just a couple of minutes away, so I asked him to wait there. I took out six thousand and when I came back I put half on his tray. I didn't say anything, after the amount of times I'd raised my offer, I knew it would just seem like another number that he would probably refuse. I just took it out just put it in front of him. I was ready to put the rest there if it even looked like he would hesitate. He didn't though, in fact you should have seen the way his eyes widened." I tell Honey with a smile. "The man stared at me, then at the money then back at me. He picked up the wads of twenties slowly and ran his thumb along the edge, fanning then to check that they were all real. Finally he nodded then reached into his pocket and took out the crystal."

Honey gasped. "Three thousand…"

"I wanted you to have that crystal," I said simply and squeezed her hand. "I bought a chain for it a few weeks later, I had to go to several jewellers looking for the perfect one before I found it, and I showed the crystal to each of them. Not a single one of them knew what it was, and that really surprised me. They all agreed that it was very rare and very expensive, but that's all."

"Yeah," Honey agreed. "The one mum went to said the same thing."

"Tempted to sell it were you?" I grin as I stir my food.

"WHAT? NEVER!!" Honey burst out, shocked. Her hand immediately going to the pendant.

"I'm sorry," I add quickly. "I didn't mean… it was a joke, a bad one I guess. Sorry."

"No, no. I'm sorry Azra," Honey replied. "Mum only took it to get it cleaned. We went to a pawn shop the day before to do it and that idiot went psycho on us over it. That really shook me up and when mum asked to borrow it, I was reluctant to part with it. I had only just found the necklace after looking so long for it, and I couldn't bear to let it out of my sight."

"Well, it's yours and no one is ever going to take it away from you." I inform her, then lean over to kiss her cheek. The smile I get in return made me feel on top of the world.

"You know," I continued after swallowing another mouthful of the risotto. "I got Paul to contact a lab to see if there was any other way to find out more about it."

"Oh? What happened?"

"They wanted to chip a piece off to test it."

"Really?" Honey exclaimed.

"Yeah," I reply. "Well, there was no way I was going to let them do that.... Does it bother you not knowing exactly what it is?"

"No. Not really, I actually kind of like that. It gives the necklace a touch of mystery." Honey smiled, enjoying her ravioli.

Dessert was gelato, Honey chose chocolate and I decided to go for strawberry. We had a lot to catch up on and we talked for so long that we ended up losing track of time, I suddenly realised that we had just a few minutes before Honey's 10pm curfew. Even as we sprinted out of the restaurant, I knew that we'd be late.

Sure enough it was twelve minutes past ten when we walked up the stairs to her porch. Honey looked at her front door for a moment then turned and slipped her arms around me.

"Today's been the first good day I've had in what seems like forever," She whispered into my chest. "I wish it didn't have to end."

"I know what you mean," I replied, holding her tight against me. Honey's hair feels so soft against my cheek, and I rubbed my face against it. She took my hand and led me to the bench beside us. "Do you think that it would be ok if I stayed awhile?" I ask when we sat.

Honey turned to me and put her hand on my chest, then leant into me and kissed my neck. "Stay forever," she breathes, her voice barely a whisper as she moved her kisses across my chin to find my lips.

“Are they still sitting out there?” John asked.

“Yup. Still on the bench,” Mary replied, looking out of the window. She let the curtain drop a second later and re-joined her husband.

“I don’t know Mary,” He added. “First she gets back late and now… maybe I should go and have a word with her.”

“Oh no you don’t,” snapped Mary. “She was only a few minutes late, and she is technically at home now. So you just leave them alone. Anyway, I'm off to bed, you coming?”

“I think I'll stay up a little longer,” John yawned.

“Uh huh,” Mary stopped at the foot of the stairs and turned to look back at her husband. “Promise me you won’t disturb them John.”

“I promise,” grumbled John as he watched his wife walk upstairs.

It was almost 2am when Mary walked back down again.

“John? Are you awake?”

“What? What time is it?” John yawned, sitting up on the couch and stretching.

“It’s almost a quarter to two,” Mary replied. “I just checked Honey’s room, its empty.”

“WHAT? They’re still out there? Right, that’s it, enough is enough.” John huffed and strode towards the door. However, before he reached it, the door opened, Azra stood there carrying Honey in his arms.

Mary gasped. “Is she ok?” She asked quickly.

“She’s just sleeping.” I reply quietly.

"I'll take her," John said, stepping forward.

"NO," I gasp, twisting away. "I.... I mean I can manage sir."

"Bring her up," called Mary from the stairs.

"Yes ma'am."

I followed Honey's mum upstairs; she pulled the covers back from the bed and began to remove Honey's shoes as I carefully lay her down so I didn't wake her. There's a wisp of hair over Honey's face and I gently brush it back as I kiss her forehead before standing and stare at her sleeping. Out of the corner of my eye I see John take a step towards me, but Mary stopped him.

"Azra?" Called Mary a moment later. "It's late, you need to be getting home."

"Yes ma'am."

"Come on son," she said softly as she took my hand and pulled me away. "You've been standing there for almost ten minutes now, it's time to go."

"Sorry," I mutter and take one last look at Honey before leaving her room.

"Did you see the way he was looking at Honey?" Giggled Mary a few minutes later.

"Yes, and I don't like it," grunted John.

"Don't be silly," Mary nudged her husband. "In fact, you should take some lessons, it's been a while since you've looked at me like that."

"What do you mean? I look at you like that all the time." John argued.

"Uh huh." Mary yawned. "Come on it's late, at least its Sunday tomorrow so we can sleep in."

"Well, you can," grumbled John. "I've got to go out early."

"Morning Honey," called Mary when she saw her daughter walking down the stairs. "How did you sleep?"

"Morning ma," Honey yawned. "Great, absolutely great, especially after so many bad nights. But I seem to have fallen asleep in my new dress. And I can't actually remember going to bed."

"That's because you fell asleep outside, and Azra carried you up."

"Really?" Honey exclaimed with a smile. "Oh, wow that's so romantic.... Wait I didn't drool, did I?"

"No," grinned Mary. "You didn't drool."

"Did I snore? Please tell me I didn't snore."

"You didn't drool, and you didn't snore," laughed Mary. "You were perfect, in fact Azra was standing over you for so long that I had to almost drag him out in the end."

"You didn't."

"I did," replied Mary. "And it's a good thing too, if I hadn't, he would probably still be standing there."

"I'm going to call him... wait, do you think it's too early? No, I'm going to call him," Honey yelled excitedly and ran back to her room.

Azra was sitting up in his bed staring at the phone when it began to vibrate in his hands.

"How did you do that?" Honey asked when I answer. "The phone didn't even ring on this end."

"I was holding it," I tell her. "I was actually wondering if I should call you."

Honey laughed, "I was just thinking the same thing a minute ago. You wanna get together if you don't have any other plans today?"

"I can be there in half an hour," I reply immediately.

"Sounds great, I'll see you in thirty." said Honey excitedly.

It's early and I don't want to disturb Paul, so I call the concierge and have him arrange a cab for me. Dropping the phone on my bed I dash to the bathroom, undressing on the way and leaving a trail of clothes behind me on my way to the shower.

About twenty-five minutes later I'm standing at Honey's front door. I check my reflection to make sure I look ok before knocking. Honey jumped into my arms as soon as she opened the door and I moan in pleasure as I squeeze her against me and lift her off the floor.

"Have you had breakfast?" She asked when I put her down.

I shook my head.

"Me neither," Honey said. "C'mon mums cooking, and she asked me to invite you if you hadn't eaten."

"Good morning Azra." Mary called from the kitchen when we walked in. "How do you like your eggs? Fried or scrambled?"

"Morning ma'am," I reply. "Anything is fine, thank you."

"Well Honey is having scrambled and I'm having mine fried, so you've got a choice."

"Fried please," I tell her as we take a seat at the table.

"Tea or coffee?" Inquired Mary. "And how do you want it?"

"Tea please, milk and two sugars if that's ok."

A few minutes later we each have plate in front of us and a stack of toast in the middle of the table. Honey let go of my hand and we all tuck in.

"So, what's your plans for today?" Asked Mary while sipping her tea.

"I haven't actually thought that far," I confess, swallowing a mouthful. I turn to Honey. "What do you think?"

"Why don't we go for a walk in the park," she suggested.

"And we can try out that sushi place for lunch," I continue.

"Then maybe a movie," finished Honey with a smile.

"Well, that was fast," chuckled Mary between mouthfuls.

"C'mon," Honey said as soon as we finish. She grabbed my hand and pulled me towards the door.

"Thanks for breakfast ma'am," I call back from the door.

The park is about a thirty-minute walk away and we're in no hurry. Small talk came effortlessly as we stroll toward it hand in hand, and in what seems like no time at all we're sitting on a bench with my arm around Honey as she rested her head on my shoulder.

"So, when were you planning on telling me that you couldn't dance?" She teased.

"Erm… well, you see…." I stutter.

"It's ok," Honey reassured me. "It's not a big deal."

"I've tried," I claim helplessly. "I even got a professional to give me lessons, I'm just no good at it."

"Don't worry about it," giggled Honey as she kissed the back of my hand. "Are there any other little secrets that you want to tell me about?"

I know what she's asking about, and I'm quiet for a few seconds before I say it. "The fight."

"Do you wanna talk about it?" Honey whispered. "It's ok if you don't."

I remove my arm from around her shoulder and turn to face her.

"What is it Azra?" She asked, a look of concern coming over her face.

"Considering everything you told me about yourself yesterday, of course I'm going to tell you about it." I trace the scar on her forearm with my finger and Honey tensed, but she didn't pull her hand away. A moment later she relaxed her arm again.

Honey took my hand in hers and squeezed it to reassure me, and I take a moment before talking.

"I have a hormone imbalance," I begin. When I see her eyes widen, I quickly add. "Don't worry It's nothing too serious. Have you ever heard of the fight or flight response?"

"Yeah, sure," Honey replied hesitantly. "It's when your body produces adrenaline to help you to run from or fight a threat."

"Exactly," I agreed. "Well in my case and in certain stressful situations the amount of adrenaline my body produces is massive. It makes me much stronger and faster, so much in fact that sometimes it can even seem like everyone else is moving at almost half their normal speed."

"Is that how you beat that guy?" She asked.

"Yeah," I nodded. "It's also why I had to change school."

"What happened?"

"We didn't always have money," I tell her. "When I started school, I was bullied…. constantly… for not having good clothes or proper trainers. It got so bad that I eventually had to end up taking self-defence classes, and that's when I realised what I could do. I thought it was normal at first and asked our sensei about it, but when I saw the funny look he gave me I quickly turned it into a joke. I started doing my own research after that, eventually I told my parents, and we went to see a doctor. He did some tests and confirmed it."

"It must have been strange to realise that no one else was going through the same thing as you", Honey declared sadly.

"Yeah, it was, but I also found some advantages. In the dojo I learnt the techniques quite easily and with my speed I was unbeatable. I advanced through the belts and things were going great; I was the star pupil and the sensei started making plans about entering me in all sorts of competitions."

"What went wrong?"

"One of the guys who used to bully me joined the dojo and I spared against him." I paused for a moment and looked around before I continued. "All those years of being bullied came out in that moment and I really tore into him. I broke his arms, one of his legs, his ribs, I smashed his jaw. They had to pull me off him Honey, and it took a lot of them to do it."

"It's ok Azra," Honey tried to reassure me, rubbing my arm.

"No Honey," I sigh softly, looking down. "It really isn't, you see I don't regret what I did to him. I hate bullies Honey, after all that time being a victim, being tormented, I hate them with a vengeance. If I could turn back time, I wouldn't change what I did. I would do the same again. Maybe I wouldn't have hurt him as badly, but I would still hurt him."

Honey wrapped her arms around me and pressed my head to her shoulder. I relax into her embrace for a few moments before lifting my head and looked at her.

"I quit the dojo that day," I continued. "There are not many things that will make me fight now Honey, and I'm vicious when I do. You may not want to be with me if you were to see just what I'm capable of."

"Now you listen to me Azra," Honey said firmly. "I don't care how bad a picture you try to paint of yourself," she put a hand on my chest. "I know who you are and you're not a bad person. And I will always be with you," she stated with absolute conviction.

I nod but wonder if Honey would still feel that way if she could actually see what I had done to that guy.

"Right. That's enough brooding," Honey suddenly declared, standing up and stepping in front of me. "Come on," she said as she took my hands and pulled me to my feet. "I'm hungry and you promised to show me how to use chopsticks."

"I don't get it," groaned Honey for what must be the fifth time.

"Look its easy just…."

"It might be easy for you Mr smarty-pants-I-pick-up-everything-so-easily." Honey pouted. "But it's not so easy for me, so stop saying that."

"Sorry…. sorry. I didn't mean it like that," I apologize quickly and took her hand in mine. "Here, rest the bottom chopstick under your thumb and on your ring finger. I put it in place on her hand. Now keep that one steady. It just rests there, there's no need for you to try and move at all. Ok?"

"Uh huh," muttered Honey uncertainly.

"Now hold the second chopstick in between your thumb, your forefinger and middle finger, like you hold a pen, yup, that's it. Ok, now move that one up and down." I release Honey's hand. Both chopsticks are moving, and you'd have to be generous to say it's up and down. "That's it, you're getting it," I encouraged her. "Now try to grab that piece of sushi."

The concentration on Honey's face is immense as she chased the sushi around the plate with her chopsticks only to have it slip between them each time. There's a look of triumph on both our faces when she finally got a grip on it and slowly lifted it up.

Honey's lips opened slightly in anticipation of her first bite and I mirror her expression. Halfway to her mouth the sushi flew out and landed on the table with a wet splat.

"That's it, I give up," Honey groaned, throwing the chopsticks on the plate. "Give me the fork."

"No no, you almost had it. Just a little…."

"At this rate lunch is going to turn into dinner," Honey grumbled. "Fork Azra. Now."

"So, what movie do you wanna watch?" I ask when we finally leave the restaurant.

"Not a si-fi," scowled Honey. "I've gone off them for a bit."

"Well, I suppose we could see that rom com if you want." I suggest.

"What, just because I'm a girl I'm supposed to like romantic comedies am I?" Accused Honey playfully.

"You do like romantic comedies," I reply. "So do I, sometimes."

"That's not the point."

"So, what is your point?" I ask.

"Umm, why does everything have to have a point?" Honey giggled. "I was just making conversation."

"Why don't we just see whatever's on the earliest." I suggested, putting my arm around her waist as we scan the list of movies.

"Erm…."

"What is it?" I ask.

"Maybe we should see the rom com," replied Honey hesitantly.

The movie was great. What we saw of it was anyway. Well, you're meant to snog in a rom-com, they are practically designed for it. So technically we were just doing what we were supposed to. We're standing in front of Honey's front door now trying to say goodnight for at least half an hour, but never quite managing it.

"Should I meet you here or at school tomorrow morning?" I ask her when I finally walk down the stairs to the lawn.

"Here," replied Honey. "If that's ok. We can walk in together."

"I'd like that," I tell her with a smile. Maybe just one more kiss, I think as I walked back up the stairs.

There must be something wrong with these clocks, I think while watching the second hand slowly drag around in circles. Time always seems to fly by whenever I'm with Honey, yet whenever I'm in class… they've done something to these clocks, I think again.

It's the last lesson of the day and these final few minutes seem to be stretching out slower and slower. Carol didn't come into school today, so Honey called her and asked if it was ok for us to come over later. We're going there straight after school. The bell finally rang and the usual mad dash for the door erupted, so I wait for it to clear before leaving myself. This classroom is at the front of the school, so I manage to get out of the building before the main surge of students. I have my bag between my legs and browse on my phone while I wait for Honey to come out. When she arrived, she grabbed me from behind and jumped onto my back. I wrap my hands around her legs and piggyback her in circles as she squealed in delight, finally putting her down when I get dizzy.

"I've behaved really badly toward Carol these last few months," Honey admitted as we make our way towards Carol's place. "We've been friends for so long, and just thinking about her leaving is hard to wrap my head around."

"Carol's a good friend," I add. "I'm sure she'll understand."

"She is," Honey agreed. "We've always been there for each other, it's just that when she told me she had asked you out I totally lost it. This friend who I loved and trusted suddenly became someone I wanted to hurt. She told me later exactly why she did it, and I do understand her reasons, but I was in a really bad place at the time and having to deal with that on top of everything else…." Honey trailed off.

"Did she tell you that she kissed me?" I ask hesitantly, deciding that it's better to deal with this little bombshell now rather than have it explode unexpectedly later.

"Yeah, she did. I really saw red with that one," Honey admitted. "If I wasn't so busy puking, I would have probably ripped her throat out right there. Yet she didn't hesitate to tell me what she did, she didn't try to hide it or lie about it and if it wasn't for her, I would never have had the courage to come and speak to you."

"Well, we both owe her for that," I reply with a smile. "It's funny how things work out sometimes."

"So, what did it feel like kissing my best friend?" Honey asked, without looking at me.

I think about that for a few second before answering. The ground seems to have suddenly gotten very slippery around me and a big mental "TREAD CAREFULLY" sign flashes in my head. "First off," I began. "I didn't kiss her, she kissed me. And it was on the cheek." I realise that this distinction doesn't make any difference to Honey, but I still feel the need to say it. "It was awkward," I continued. "She did apologise immediately after it happened, but I left straight away. I wasn't sure what her intentions were when she asked me out, but I was still quite annoyed that she did. Especially since she was your best friend."

Honey nodded. "When I didn't tell her about why we broke up, she went to you to try and find out. She thought that the only way she could help me was if she could find out the reason for our breakup. She didn't really fancy you, but after that fight you had, she saw something in you that she hadn't seen before. Carol has a bit of a thing for bad boys."

We arrived at Carol's door and Honey gave me a quick hug before knocking. A moment later Carol opened the door and stared at Honey.

"Yes?" She inquired blandly.

Honey looked at the floor. "I'm sorry I've been a bit of a jerk lately, I know I've …."

"Ok," Carol laughed as she leaped at Honey and hugged her. "Come on in. Sorry about the mess," she gestured around at the cardboard boxes scattered around. "We're in the middle of packing."

She went to the fridge and took out three cans of cola, then handed Honey one. "It's polite to offer your guests a drink when you have one," she stated pointedly when she held the other can out for me.

"Sorry," I mumbled, taking the can from her.

"Where is everyone?" Asked Honey, glancing around.

"Dads getting the new place sorted, and mums out shopping," Carol replied, walking into her room. "I've packed almost everything away," she waved a hand around the spotless room. "There's only a few bits and pieces left and a couple of outfits."

"You're not coming back to school, are you?" Stated Honey gloomily.

"No… mums already told the school we're leaving." Carol replied sadly. "Dad said that it's coming up to the end of the financial year, the one time when accountants are in demand. He's been counting on this being his best chance on finding another job, and he can't afford to let it pass".

"I'm going to miss you so much," Honey sobbed as she hugged Carol.

"Me too Hon, me too."

I walk out and go to the living room to give them a few moments. It's over an hour before they come out again.

"I'm sorry I called you a coward Hon," Carol apologised as she walked us to the front door. "I know it must have felt like a slap in the face to hear me say it."

"Yeah, yeah it was." Honey admitted. "But don't be sorry, it turned out to be exactly what I needed to knock some sense into me."

"That's what I hoped," Carol replied. "I know that your mum is really cool and that she would have probably been really supportive with everything you were going through, but you still hadn't spoken to Azra. I had this thought at the time that what you really needed was a good hard kick in the butt to set you straight. I knew that you may never speak to me again because of it, but I figured that it would be worth the risk."

"Well it worked," Honey agreed with a little laugh. "So, thank you for the figurative slap in the face and the kick in the butt."

"Hey, don't knock it," Carol teased in mock seriousness. "Sometimes all the hugs and kind words in the world don't count for much when what you really need is a bit of tough love."

"Right, anyway! I want you to call me as soon as you get there," Honey stated, giving Carol a hug at the door. "And we need to make plans for us to visit as soon as possible."

Honey leaned against my arm when Carol closed the door behind us. "I'm glad you're here Azra," she said softly. "I don't know what I would have done if I had lost both you and Carol."

I'm Not Afraid

It's been a couple of weeks since Carol moved out, Honey's been trying to keep a brave face, but having moved schools myself I know exactly how hard it is to lose your best friend. There's not a lot I can do except be there for her. I settle my hair in the reflection of the window before knocking on Honey's front door.

"C'mon in," smiled Mary when she opened the door. "Honey's not down yet, would you like a cup of tea?"

"Thank you ma'am," I reply, taking a seat at the dining table. "That would be great... Erm I realise that I've been coming here a lot...well pretty much every day for a while. I hope I'm not making a nuisance of myself."

Honey's dad grunted, and I look at the floor embarrassed.

"Ignore him," Mary said as she elbowed her husband. "He's always this grumpy, and don't be silly, you're more than welcome here."

"MA," called Honey, running down the stairs, "Azra will be here soon I don't want him to..." she froze as soon as she saw me. With a yelp and a no no no no, Honey turned and ran back up the stairs.

I'm out of the chair and after her like a shot. "Honey?" I call, taking the stairs two at a time, only to have her bedroom door shut in my face a second before I can reach her.

"Honey, is everything ok?" I ask, knocking on her door. The urge to just barge in is so strong that I have to hold the doorframe to stop myself.

"Yeah, yeah everything's fine Azra." She replied rather too hurriedly. "Can you wait for me downstairs please?"

I hear her rushing around the room muttering, but I can't make out any of the words. I know that her door has no lock and I reach for the handle, but stop myself and knock again. "Sure Honey, but I'm getting a bit worried here. I just need to know that you're ok....Please..." The desperation in my voice stopped her, because everything went silent. After a few long seconds I hear her right on the other side of the door.

"My phone ran out of battery Azra, I overslept. I haven't had a shower, or brushed my hair, I'm still in my pj's. I haven't even brushed my teeth. I... I don't want you to see me like this."

Relief floods through me and I rest my head on the doorframe. "Oh Honey, don't you get it yet?" I whisper. "None of that stuff matters to me. I don't care how long you haven't combed your hair or been wearing your pyjamas. I don't care how long you haven't brushed your teeth...." I stop on that. "Actually Honey, brush your teeth. Good oral hygiene is healthy, but the rest of it doesn't mean anything to me. Dressing up is fine when we go out, but I don't want you to feel that you must do it just for me."

The door opened and Honey stood there with her head hanging down. "I just want to look my best; I don't want you to..." she trailed off.

"I know," I reply, embracing her. "I'm always checking myself in your front window before I knock. And you Honey...." I take a step back and raise her chin to face me.... "You have never looked more perfect than you do right now."

That night when Honey walked in Mary was in the living room watching tv.

"Hi ma," Honey greeted cheerily and sat down beside her mother. "Watcha watching?"

"Just some reality show," Mary replied. "How was your day?"

"Pretty great actually," Honey smiled. "We decided to try indoor rock climbing, it was really cool. Not something I would have thought of to do, but it was fun."

"I worry about you being out this late."

"It's not yet ten ma, I'm back before my curfew."

"I know Honey, I just worry when you're out late. Especially with you wearing that necklace."

"I'm never taking it off ma," Honey replied defensively, her hand going straight to her neck. "Besides I'm always with Azra, and he's more than capable taking care of any trouble. We had these guys acting funny a few days ago…" Honey trailed off.

"What guys?" Mary inquired, raising her eyebrows and turning towards her daughter.

"It wasn't anything really," Honey replied quickly as she got off the sofa.

"Honey, what happened?" Mary insisted.

"It wasn't anything important ma," Honey yawned dismissively. "We were at the bar Carol's dad worked in, some guys started acting funny and Azra took care of it. Anyway, I'm off to bed, I'll see you in the morning."

Mary stared at her daughters back all the way up the stairs until it disappeared behind her bedroom door. Not at all convinced with Honey's blasé response, in fact the overly casual reaction that she had suddenly adopted actually increased Mary's interest rather than deflecting it. Mary decided to pay the place a visit after work the next day.

Rough looking place she thought after walking in and looking around, there were several small round tables, each with four old wooden chairs around them. On the wall to her left was a large jukebox that looked like it had stood there for years, and a pool table on the right. The bar took up most of the wall at the far end, and the smell of frying drifted across from the kitchen that was behind it.

"Hello," Mary smiled, walking around the tables and taking a seat at the bar.

"Hey, what can I get you?" The woman behind the counter offered.

"Jack Danial's please. Straight, no ice," Mary replied. "Nice place."

"Liar," the bartender announced candidly, but had a smile on her face when she said it.

"Why don't you have one yourself while you're at it," Mary offered.

"Very kind of you, thanks." The bartender nodded and poured out two shots.

"Cheers," said Mary and downed the shot in one go.

"Woah, easy there," the bartender laughed. But not to be outdone she did the same.

"I needed that, another two please." Mary grinned and pushed the glass across the bar. "Cheers."

Mary sipped from the second glass, but she still finished it in a couple of minutes.

"I'm Mary," she said clinking the third glass with the bartender. Mary brought the glass up but just let the liquid touch her lips before bringing it back down again. She held the glass in her fist to hide how much was still in it.

"Jane," the bartender introduced herself as she took a gulp.

Mary pretended to take another sip, then lowered her hand to her lap. Hidden from view by the bar she tilted the glass and let the amber liquid pour out onto the floor, to be lost among the other accidental spillages. Mary brought the empty glass back up to her lips and upended it as she threw her head back.

“Keep em coming,” Mary smiled, sliding the empty glass across the bar, she knew that there was no chance of getting a bartender drunk, but maybe just tipsy enough to loosen her tongue.

“So, what brings you here Mary?” Jane asked as they started on their fourth glass. “We don’t see many new faces in this place.”

“Friend of mine told me a funny story,” Mary lied. Still pretending to drink, once again she discretely emptied the whiskey onto the floor.

“I like funny stories,” Jane laughed heartily, taking a sip. “How does this one go?”

“He said you had a bit of a fight out here.”

“You a cop?” Jane snapped, the humour in her voice vanishing in a second as she stared across the bar.

“God no,” Mary snorted, putting the empty glass back on the bar. The change in the bartender’s demeanour was very abrupt, but Mary had been expecting something like it. “Though after what he told me, I just had to come down and find out for myself. Bit of a sucker for the unusual,” Mary picked up the refilled glass and stared at the contents for a moment, she lifted her head slightly and looked at Jane, a small smile at the end of her lips.

“Oh? What’s so unusual about a fight?” Jane asked carefully.

“Nothing normally, Mary muttered softly. A hint of conspiracy in her voice. Except when it involves a teenage boy. Who also happened to win... Did you see it?” Mary leaned forward eagerly. She took a sip from the glass; Jane was watching too closely to pretend anymore.

“Yeah, I saw it.” Jane replied.

“God, I wish I had.” Mary sighed, looking up at the ceiling, she swirled the amber liquid around in the glass, then took a mouthful and leaned forward again. "How did it go down?" Mary whispered excitedly, her eyes wide.

Jane looked around the bar then across into Mary's expectant face, she took a sip of the whiskey. "He was with a girl, pretty blonde thing she was. They were sitting down there." The bartender pointed to a table....

Azra took a sip from the glass of cola and looked across the table at Honey. She had insisted that we come and have a look at the place after I told her about Carol bringing me here.

"She didn't play fair," I pointed across to the pool table. "Made a comment about my butt just when I took my shot, made me miss."

Honey smiled. "Yeah, she told me about it. That's Carol all right," she admitted.

"Well, it wouldn't have been very funny if I had actually ripped a hole in the table though." I mutter.

"She beat you?" Honey teased.

"By not playing fair," I reply defensively. "I should have won that game."

"Can you teach me how to play?" Honey asked. "I've never played pool before. Hell, I've never been in a bar before."

"Sure, if you want." I patted my pockets trying to find some change. "Bars that serve food can allow under eighteens in, but I think the only reason that the bartender let us stay is because we know Carol."

"Azra, there's a guy behind you that keeps looking at us," Honey pointed with her chin. "He's been doing it for a while now."

I turn and look where Honey had indicated. "Dammit," I curse, turning back, I knew it was a bad idea coming here. "That's the guy I had the fight with."

“Him?” Honey gasped. “He’s huge.”

I look over my shoulder again, two more guys have joined him and all three of them are looking at us now.

“I think it’s time to leave,” I tell Honey and stand up.

“Uh huh,” she agreed quickly, getting up as well and we walked towards the exit.

I can feel their eyes on me as we crossed the room, and I hear three sets of chairs move when they get up behind us. “Turn right as soon as we’re outside,” I whisper. “They’re not interested in you.”

“I'm not leaving you Azra.” Honey insisted.

“Listen to me Honey, I can handle this but only if I know that you're safe. If I'm worrying about you, I'm going to get hurt. Do you trust me?”

“Of course I do, but…”

“Go right,” I repeat urgently. “Don’t come out till it’s over.”

Honey nodded and did what I ask as we exit the bar. I wish that I was as confident as I sound. I’ve never fought more than two people at a time, and that was sparring with guys my age in the safety of the dojo.

There’s a guy getting off his bike ahead of me. He looked behind me to the bar for a moment and nodded, then back at me and his eyes narrowed.

Damn, I can't afford to be trapped between them, so I head straight towards the new guy, I feel the surge of adrenaline as it hits me, and I quicken my step. He doesn’t have a clue what to expect so he doesn’t react as I walk right up to him and headbutt him in the face then kick him in the nuts. He fell to his knees, and I spin on the ball of my left foot and brought the right across his temple. He’s not getting up so it’s back to three again.

Morello's two friends split up as they advance on me, the one on the left went around the line of motorcycles so that they can come at me from both sides. The guy on the right is closer so I head towards him. He threw a punch which I easily sidestepped and slammed my right palm into his nose breaking it, then punch his ribs with my left Followed by a kick behind his knee to sweep him off his feet and knock him on his back. He just needs to be stunned long enough for me to deal with lefty.

I hear lefty behind me and turn in time to see him swing a knife. A simple step back took me out of his reach, and I grab his wrist then smash the palm of my other hand into the back of his elbow, making his arm bend in the opposite way of what it's supposed to as something inside snapped. The knife fell out of his useless hand, and I snatch it out of the air then shove it into his thigh. As his leg gave out, I use his own momentum to grab the guy's head with both hands and slam my knee into his face. That's two down for the count, I quickly glance around for Morello. I see him edging along on my left, but he hasn't come any closer.

Typical bully I think, before turning back to broken nose as I watch him get up and carefully walk towards me. His eyes are watering from my earlier blow and the tears obscure his vision as he threw a clumsy punch. I don't even bother dodging; I block his swing and bring my right foot down hard on his ankle breaking it. After he collapsed, I reach down and lift his arm, I look up at Morello as I step on his friend's chest and begin twisting his arm. The guy under me started screaming in pain but I ignore him, keeping eye contact with Morello the whole time while I twist. When the snap finally came it isn't loud, but I see Morello jerk back. I finally let the arm go and start walking towards him.

Morello's eyes darted around to his fallen friends, and he pulled out a knife while walking backwards. He waved it around the air like it's some sort of talisman. I'm in no hurry as I follow, I want his fear to build, I want this bully to feel the fear that he is so used to instilling in others.

Morello has backed up into a tree now, but I don't think that he even realises this as his legs are still moving. When I came up to him, he took a proper swing at me with his knife. I grabbed his hand mid-swing with my right and threw a hard punch to his ribs with my left, I feel them break and he almost fell. But I'm not done yet, so I lift him back upright by his chin. Both my hands are occupied and the last thing I want is for him to punch me. I may not feel it right now, but I will when the adrenaline in me vanishes. I squeezed his chin hard hoping that he tries to pull my hand away, and that's exactly what he does.

"This is the second time we've met," I tell Morello, while forcing his knife hand up towards his face. "Since there isn't going to be a third let's have a little fun." He shut his eyes tight and tried to turn his face away when he realised how close the tip of the blade is to his eye.

"Open your eyes, or I'll cut your eyelids off," I growl menacingly. Morello's eyes shot open, and his pupils enlarge as he stared at me in fear.

"You know, I've always wondered what would happen when your eye pops out and is hanging down your cheek. Would you still be able to see out of it? Would one eye be seeing your feet, and the other straight ahead? What do you think that would be like? I think maybe it's time to find out."

"So which eyeball do you want to keep?" I ask while brushing the tip of his knife against his lashes. He goes cross eyed trying to look at me and the knife and I suddenly slam my forehead into his mouth. Morello's head doesn't have anywhere to go with the tree behind it and I feel most of his teeth break.

I turn and walk away; it takes a second before I hear him collapse behind me. I have my eyes on the floor when I walk back, I don't need to look to see the carnage around me. I know exactly what I've done. Did they deserve it? Four grown men against one sixteen-year-old… Hell yeah, they deserved it. My only regret is that Honey watched me do it, but she needed to know exactly what I'm capable of. Will she… can she accept me now? I don't know, but I'm about to find out as I see her step out from among the small group of wide-eyed onlookers who have gathered outside the bar. I have my face down the whole time as she walked towards me.

Honey stood in front of me for a second, then lifted my chin up to look in my eyes. She slid her arms around my chest and whispered, "I'm not afraid."

I release the breath I didn't realise I was holding and hug her back, a few seconds later she took my hand and led me away from the broken men laying around us.

"Damn," Mary muttered in astonishment.

"I ended up calling the ambulance instead of the cops," Jane finished. "Told them that those guys must have had some sort of falling out between themselves. What else could I say? Who would believe it? They'll start wondering just what the hell we're serving here."

"Do you know what hospital they were taken to?" Mary asked before she left.

"Good morning Azra." Mary said, rather too casually when she opened the door for me the next morning. "Sit with me a moment will you." She continued as she walked to the dining table.

"Yes ma'am," I took the chair opposite her, and she stared at me rather pointedly while sipping her tea. "Is something wrong ma'am?" I ask after several minutes.

"Well," Mary began. "I'm trying to connect two pictures together and having a bit of difficulty, so maybe you can help me. The first is of a quiet, polite young man sitting in front of me. And the second is four brutally injured men lying in hospital beds."

Damn, I think looking down at the table. Honey told me that she let slip about the fight, but also that she didn't give her mum any details. How does she know there were four? What else does she know? Should I say something? She hasn't actually asked me anything, maybe I should wait.......Ok she still isn't talking, this is starting to feel weird. I should say something. No, count to thirty then do it. But what should I say? Don't wanna try and justify myself, that always comes out making you look guilty. Maybe I....

"How did you do it?" Mary finally asked.

"Adrenaline." I answer quickly, relieved that I wasn't the first to speak. "My body can produce a lot of it in certain situations."

She nodded. "Do you enjoy fighting?"

"No," I answer truthfully. I don't mention the satisfaction I felt giving those bullies a taste of their own medicine.

"Why did you do it?"

"Do what?" I retort, rather more loudly than I intend. "Why did I defend myself? Or why did I not let them assault me?"

"Why did you have to hurt them so badly?" Mary asked desperately.

"Would you have preferred if Azra had slapped their wrist and told them not to do it again?" Honey interrupted from the stairs. "And maybe we should also hope that they don't hurt the next person they assault too badly."

Honey continued down then sat beside me and put her hand over mine.

"One of them had been harassing Carol from the day her dad started working there," Honey went on as she stared across the table at her mother. "Azra didn't pick this fight, so don't you judge him. And it will be a long time before that lot will be picking on anyone again... if they ever do."

Honey kept eye contact with her mother for a minute before standing up.

“Come on Azra, we’re done here,” Honey stated coldly and pulled me towards the door.

Mary silently watched them leave.

“I can't believe that she tried to corner you with that,” Honey grumbled when we’re outside. “I’m so sorry that I mentioned it, it just slipped out when she was telling me how worried she was, I didn’t mean to…”

“It’s ok,” I reassure her quickly. “You were pretty cool in there.”

“You think so?” Honey’s lips curled up in a smile. “Well, I wasn’t going to just let her talk to you like that.”

Taking a stand

It's been over a month since our confrontation with Honey's mum, and she hasn't ever mentioned it again. I felt really awkward when I visited the next day and had suggested to Honey that maybe I shouldn't come over for a bit but she wasn't having any of that. Honey was adamant that if there were any issues, we would deal with them now rather than tiptoe around her mother.

It was therefore rather surprising that Mary acted like nothing happened and went back to treating me the same as she had before. Which is cool considering the amount of time I spend there.

Honey asked me earlier if we could visit our spot on the hill and we're on our way there right now. It's a warm clear night and all the stars are visible, perfect for stargazing.

"Thanks Paul," Honey said, picking up the blanket we brought with us as she got out of the car.

Paul nodded at Honey with a smile then looked across at me.

"Might as well head home," I tell him.

As we walk the rest of the way I took the blanket from Honey, and she snuggled against my arm. "You picked a perfect night," I tell her as we unfold the blanket and lie back on it.

There isn't a single cloud around tonight, and it's like someone has scattered millions of tiny diamonds across the heavens as the stars twinkle in the sky. Up here all alone it feels like we're the only two people in the world. Honey has one hand in mine and the other on her necklace as we gaze up.

"You've been awfully quiet for the longest time," I whisper to her. "Is everything ok?"

Honey sat up and looked at me for a moment. "The last time we were up here, you gave me something special," she said slowly. "Now I want to give you something."

"Oh, what's that?" I smile, sitting up as well.

Honey looked away nervously and started blushing.

It takes me a minute to realise just what she means, and my jaw drops open. "Oh…. You mean…"

"If… if you want to that is, she whispered softly… "You've never mentioned it, I don't know if you've thought about it…"

"Yes," I blurt out rather faster than I wanted to. "I have, I've thought about it... I… I mean I do want to… erm…"

I've been waiting for this moment all my life, and now that it's here I have absolutely no clue what I should do next. I look at Honey with what must be the dumbest expression on my face as I try to think of something cool to say or do. Unfortunately, all coherent thought seems to have fled and I just sit here, frozen… I think my mouth is still hanging open and I shut it quickly.

Honey touched my cheek and slid her thumb across my lips, then moved her hand behind my neck and pulled me towards her. When our lips touch the world around me disappears and then nothing else mattered.

Honey lay in bed with one arm behind her head and a huge smile across her face as she replayed the events of the previous night in her mind. Her smile getting wider with each repetition. Eventually there's a knock on the door, but Honey doesn't even hear it. After a few seconds there's another knock and her mother opened the door.

"Oh, you're awake," Mary said, walking in. "My, you do look pleased with yourself," she smiled as she opened the curtains.

“Morning ma,” Honey sighed.

“You look like the cat that caught the canary,” Mary went on, walking towards Honey. “In fact… you're practically… glowing.” The last few words coming out slowly as she looked her daughter in the eye.

Oh damn, thought Honey as she turned away. Mary took Honey’s head in her hands and stared at her daughter’s face, Honey was still smiling, she’s unable to stop.

“You didn’t???” Mary muttered hesitantly, turning Honey’s face around to look at it... “Oh God, you did!!” She gasped, suddenly letting go and Honey’s head bounced back onto the pillow.

“AZRA!!” She spat his name out. “That little bastard,” snarled Mary, standing.

“HEY, don’t you call him that,” Honey snapped, jumping to her feet.

“That son of a bitch, just wait till I get my hands on him….”

“Don’t you dare talk about him like that,” Honey yelled, scrambling after her mother.

“Thinks he can do that to my daughter and get away with it, I’ll wring his bloody….”

“HEY.” This time Honey grabbed her mother’s hand and forced her around. “It was my idea,” Honey yelled straight into her face.

“What…??” Mary stuttered. Finally focusing on her daughter.

“It was my idea.” Honey repeated.

“You…??” Mary was in full berserker mode and has trouble changing course. “Are you lying to protect him?” Her eyes narrowed as she glared at Honey.

“No.” Honey stated simply, staring back. “Azra’s never once mentioned sex.”

“Then why…??” Mary pleaded.

“This conversation is over unless you apologise for calling Azra those names.” Honey announced icily. “I won’t have you talking about him like that.”

“Oh,” Mary, sat down on Honey’s bed looking lost. “Oh,” she repeated. She looked around the room blankly then back at Honey. “I'm sorry,” she finally murmured a minute later.

Honey sat down beside her mother and they both stared at the wall for a while.

“Why?” Mary asked again.

“Why do you think…??” Honey replied nervously. “I’ve wanted to for ages, even before we broke up. I just didn’t have the guts to before.”

“Oh,” Mary said yet again and they both go back to staring at the wall. “Why didn’t you talk to me? You didn’t have to rush into such a big decision.”

“Would you have tried to talk me out of it?” Honey asked quietly, turning her gaze down to the floor.

Mary looked at her for a minute. “Maybe,” she finally admitted.

“That’s why I didn’t come to you. It would have been nice to talk to someone, but I didn’t want to be lectured and I didn’t want to be talked out of it. Both of which you would have done if I came to you.” Honey turned to her mother and reached out to hold her hand. “It would have only caused an argument between us ma, and I didn’t want an argument to overshadow something as important…as… as amazing as this.”

“I just think you could have waited a bit longer,” Mary stammered hesitantly.

“For how much longer?” Honey sighed. “A week? A month? When would it have been a good time for you? I didn’t rush into this ma.”

“Well, he better have used protection,” Mary blurted out a minute later.

“Hah,” Honey choked. “He didn’t even know it was going to happen until.... well...,” Honey stared at her feet again before she continued. “I started taking the pill three weeks ago,” she whispered.

“WHAT?” Mary gasped, spinning around to face Honey. “The pill... Three weeks??”

“That’s when I first decided to... you know. I wanted it to be on the hill where he gave me my necklace.” Honey explained. Her hand was at her neck, and she twisted the crystal around her thumb and forefinger as she continued. “I had to wait that long for the perfect night.”

“Well,” Mary said finally, staring at Honey wide eyed. “This is not to say I approve, because I don’t. But you better not let your father find out or he’ll stop you seeing Azra.”

“No... he won’t,” Honey replied coldly.

“Excuse me?”

“I said, no he won’t,” Honey stared back at her mother, wondering how she could even suggest such a thing...

“I don’t like the tone of your voice young lady.” Mary stated in a low voice.

“I'm sorry ma I don’t mean to be rude when I say this, but you need to understand something. I lost him once; I won’t let it happen again. Azra Belongs To Me!! He's mine, and I won’t give him up... for anyone.” The steel in her voice didn’t surprise Honey, she meant every single word.

Mary looked at Honey for a few seconds, a strange expression on her face. Then she put her palm on Honey’s cheek and gently moved her thumb across. “Don’t let your father know,” she said quietly before getting up and walking out.

“I can't find any Azra,” Honey yelled out, holding the fridge door open. “I think you’ve run out.”

“There should be another case in the cabinet to the left of the oven,” I call back while scrolling through an endless list of movies on the tv. I turn to look at Honey while she searched through the cupboards in my kitchen. Having her here in my apartment is absolutely amazing, and I rest my chin on the back of the sofa as I stare at her in wonder.

“Got it,” Honey replied, taking out a twelve pack of colas. After putting two bottles aside, she emptied the rest into the fridge. “Where’s the bottle opener?”

“There should be one in the drawer above where the colas were.” I point while still watching her. I've never had a problem living alone, in fact I've gotten quite used to it. Yet until now I didn’t ever realise just how empty the apartment was, that is till Honey filled it with her presence.

Honey came back with two open bottles and held one out for me.

“Thanks,” I smile, taking it and having a sip.

“Why don’t you just get cans instead of bottles?” Honey asked, settling down beside me. “That way you won’t need to keep looking for an opener.”

“When I was little, I would watch these soft drink ads on tv,” I began. “They would always have bottles and I loved the way the condensation would drip down the side. We couldn’t afford to buy bottles then. Well, I supposed we could, but it would mean giving up something more important for them. Anyway, since then I've always thought of them as being a bit of a luxury item.”

“Haven’t you decided on a movie yet?” Honey grumbled, snuggling closer and wrapping my arm around herself.

“There’s just so many to choose from,” I shrug and turned my attention back to the tv. “I’ve already seen all the good ones.”

"Uh huh," Honey mumbled while I continue to scroll through the lists. "You know sometimes I think my mother has some sort of mind reading skill. She just looked at me that morning and seemed to know straight away."

"How do you feel about her knowing about it?" Honey and I have talked about this before, but the subject has come up a couple of times in the few days since our night together.

"I'm fine with it," she answered. "Not so long ago I would have been terrified about her finding out. Now, not so much." Honey shrugged indifferently. "Just deal with it and move on."

"That's a huge difference in reactions," I tell her.

"I know," Honey admitted. "And I've wondered about it myself. It's just that after all the horror and despair that I went through when I lost you, it put a lot of things in perspective. And now that I have you back, well.... Things that were scary before, don't seem quite so scary anymore."

"And your mum knows that you're here at my place?"

"Yup, I told her this morning that I was coming here with you after school." Honey replied with a grin.

"And you're sure she was ok with it?" I ask, yet again.

"Actually, I'm not sure." Honey admitted, her smile turning into a frown. "Like I said, I told her I was coming here. I wasn't asking for her permission, and I think she knew the difference. It seems like there's a whole new set of dynamics for us at the moment, and we're both kinda finding our way around. Don't worry," Honey patted my thigh. "We'll work it out."

"And your dad?"

"That," Honey sighed. "Is a totally different issue. She told me not to say anything to him, and I haven't. He doesn't even know I'm here; he would flip if he did. But to be honest since he's going to find out eventually, I would prefer to just get it all out into the open and deal with it now, rather than worry about dealing with it later. Anyway, you've had your chance. Give me the remote, I'm going to choose the movie."

"Do you know what that is?" John snarled, throwing an empty blister pack of tablets on the coffee table in front of Mary. "Birth control," he continued without waiting for a reply. "THAT SON OF A BITCH HAS MY DAUGHTER ON THE DAMN PILL."

"Where did you find that?" Mary asked quietly.

"Where the hell do you think I found it? She hadn't emptied her bin, so I had to get it, it was right there," John fumed, stalking back and forth. "Right there on top of her thrash. I was worried about what it was, so I looked the name up. The Pill.... The damn Pill."

"Listen to me John, you need to calm down...."

"WHAT??...CALM DOWN? How the hell can you say that," John suddenly froze midstride and turned to stare at his wife in horror... "YOU KNEW!!" He stammered. "When? Why didn't you tell me?"

"A month ago. And I knew how you would react, to be fair I pretty much reacted the same way. Anyway, I decided it was something we needed to sort out woman to woman."

"WHAT? Woman to... Honey's not a woman! She's sixteen, she's still a child. It's HIM, it's his fault. Somehow that pervert has managed to talk her into.... Just you wait till I get my hands on that scumbag."

"NO!! Don't you touch him." Mary burst out, jumping up. "I've spoken to Honey; it's been dealt with."

"Dealt with?? You think something like this can be sorted with a simple conversation? I going to rip his damn head off." Roared John, slamming his fist into his palm.

"That's Enough!!" Shouted Mary. "Don't you even think of going near him. I told you I've already spoken to Honey about this."

Something in Mary's voice caused John to pause and look at his wife. He turned to face her. "Right… Right, you've spoken to her," he repeated slowly. "So, now it's my turn to speak to him then."

"What do you mean?" Mary asked cautiously.

"A talk, that's all," muttered John.

"Fine, talk to him." Mary said firmly. "But that's it."

"Uh huh, just a little chat. Man to man," John spat out that last word distastefully.

As soon as the front door opened that evening, John jumped off the sofa and called out, "Honey can you ask Azra to come in for a moment, I need to have a word with him."

"Sure dad", Honey replied, holding the door open. "Azra, can you come in, dad wants to speak to you."

I turn and nod then walk back towards the house. Honey's hand is still on the door, and I brush mine against it gently when I go past her.

"Hello sir," I smile. "What can I…" I don't finish my sentence before I'm grabbed and slammed against the wall.

"No," yelled Mary, jumping up.

"DAD", screamed Honey hysterically, trying to pull him off.

Mary watched, horrified. Her body frozen as John's fist smashed Azra's face down. When Azra looked up, he made eye contact with Mary for a second. Then John battered him down again. When his head came up this time Azra's lip is split open and blood runs down his chin, he stared at Mary again until the next blow slammed his head down. Now blood is streaming down his nose, but this time Azra wasn't looking at Mary anymore. Mary followed Azra's gaze just in time to see Honey swing the chair.

"LET HIM GO DAMN YOU!!" screamed Honey, swinging the chair into her father's back.

John finally released me, and we both collapsed to the floor.

"OHGOD OHGOD," sobbed Honey, rushing to me. There's nothing else to hand so she used her blouse to try to wipe the blood on my face.

"HOW COULD YOU?" Honey screamed at her father as Mary helped him to his feet, then turned back to me. "I'm here Azra," she coaxed gently. "I'm here. Can you stand?"

"Uh huh," I nod slowly, blood splashing from my chin to the floor. Honey used her hand to wipe my face, then brushed the blood off on her skirt.

"I've got you." Honey encouraged, putting my hand across her shoulders. Using the wall for leverage I slowly manage to get back on my feet. "C'mon let's get you out of here," Honey urged. I leave bloody handprints on the wall when I use it for support as we stagger towards the door.

"Can you wait here a minute?" Honey asked, helping me into the bench outside the front door. "I need to have a word with my father, then we can leave."

"Uh huh."

"What the hell is wrong with you?" Honey burst back in, slamming the front door open.

"Don't you raise your voice at me young lady!" Yelled John, standing up and striding up to her. "You listen to me…"

"NO," interrupted Honey, staring her father down. "You listen to me. I'm leaving now, and if you ever want to see me again, you're going to apologise to Azra for what you just did."

"You're not going anywhere," bellowed John, grabbing Honey's hand. "The only place you're going is to your room."

"Let. Go. Of. Me." Stated Honey coldly, her words are not loud but the conviction in her voice caused her father to pause.

"I think we've given you way too much freedom..." John stammered, trying to fall back on the authority of being a father.

"John," shouted Mary, jumping between them. "You need to let go of Honey now."

"I'm not going to just let her walk out of here Mary," argued John. "I'm putting a stop to this nonsense right now."

"You ok Honey?" I call out, holding the front door open.

"You stay right there young man," ordered Mary. "Don't you come any closer."

"Yes ma'am," I replied. "Honey...??"

"I'm fine Azra," reassured Honey. "I'll be with you in a minute."

"Ok Honey," I nod and step back out, closing the door behind me.

"John.... Please.... let go of Honey." Begged Mary, turning her attention back to her husband.

"What's wrong?" Asked John, finally letting go of Honey and reaching for his wife. "Did you think I was-going to hit her? You know I would never do that."

"I know you wouldn't," Mary began.

"Hey, where do you think you're going?" John yelled, seeing Honey walk towards the door. He moved past Mary to stop her.

"Let her go John," said Mary, taking his hand and holding him back. "Let her go."

"You talk to him ma." Honey called from the door before closing it behind her.

"Come on Azra, let's go." She held my hand as we walked towards the waiting car.

"What the hell? Shouted John. "Are you going to just let her leave?"

"Sit down John." Mary went to the kitchen and took out two glasses and a bottle of whiskey. After pouring an inch into each glass, she brought them into the living room and gave one to John.

"What's going on Mary?" Demanded John, putting his glass on the table untouched.

"What the hell do you think we should have done?" Snapped Mary angrily. "Locked her up in her room? Then what? Keep her there? Don't you realise that as soon as she turned 16, she can legally leave this house and never come back. Is that what you want her to do?"

"No of course not." John replied. "But I'm just trying to look out for her."

"How John? By forcing her to stay? That would have just made her resent you…resent us even more. Anyway, Azra would never have let you, one word from Honey and he would have had her out of here in a minute."

"Azra?" Muttered John, confused.

"You may not have noticed while you were busy bashing his head in," added Mary. "But he didn't make a single move to even try to stop you. He kept his hands to his sides the whole time."

"What are you talking about?" Said John, the look of confusion on his face spreading. "He's a sixteen-year-old kid, what do you think he could have done?"

"He could have stopped you any time he wanted," replied Mary, taking a sip from the glass. "The only reason he didn't is because you're Honey's father."

"I have absolutely no idea what you're talking about." John picked up his glass and stood. "You've totally lost me."

"Azra knows how to fight John, and he's very good at it." Answered Mary. "He's already put four guys in the hospital."

"You're worried after some playground brawl he had?"

"It wasn't just some playground brawl with other kids," explained Mary testily. "They were bikers, and one of them was bigger than you." Mary told her husband everything that she found out at the bar.

"Impossible," said John disbelievingly, when she finished. "Azra? He's always so.... polite. It can't have been him."

"I know, that's what I thought too," continued Mary. "So, I found out which hospital they were taken to and went there. I couldn't believe what that bartender told me, I had to see for myself."

"And?" Said John, taking a gulp of the whiskey. "Did you?"

Mary nodded slowly. "I thought that the story was bad, but it was even worse seeing them. They were wrapped up like mummies, full body casts on two of them. Arms, legs broken, one of them had all his front teeth smashed in, just a gaping hole and jagged edges of a few teeth left. His lips cut up and swollen almost more than double, he had to eat through a straw."

"God," muttered John, finishing his glass.

"I asked him what happened, who did this to him. He thought I was a cop and told me to get lost, he could barely talk John. But I needed to know so I showed him a photo of Azra from my phone."

"Did he recognize him?" Asked John.

"He freaked out, started screaming for the doctors and pushing buttons on all the machines around him. He was terrified, absolutely terrified."

John brought the glass to his lips and realising it was empty, put it down again. He looked around blankly for a moment. Mary offered him the glass she was holding, and he took it gratefully.

"I wasn't afraid you were going to hit Honey," Admitted Mary. "I was worried what Azra would do if he thought you were going to hurt her."

"Is that why you let her go? Because you were afraid of him?" John accused, staring at his wife.

"Don't be stupid!!" Snapped Mary immediately … "Sorry, sorry. I didn't mean to call you that. I'm surprised that you would think that I'd let anyone take my daughter if she didn't want to go. I wouldn't, no matter what they were capable of."

Mary took the empty glass and went to the bottle of whiskey. After pouring herself some she came back to the couch and sat down.

"Azra was willing to take a beating for her, and Honey was willing to attack you for him…." Mary paused to take a sip from her glass. "Trying to keep them apart after what you did would have just started another fight. And that would have accomplished nothing, except broken us all further apart. If we had tried to force her to stay, it would have only pushed her further away. No John, there's only one way to get Honey back. You're going to have to apologise to Azra."

"WHAT...? NO," yelled John, jumping up and shaking his head, the contents of his glass spilling over his hands. "There's no way in hell I'm going to apologise to some kid after he's slept with my daughter," John snarled adamantly, putting the glass on the table and wiping his hands on his shirt.

"Now you listen to me," ordered Mary. "I warned you not to touch him, but you didn't listen. I'm not willing to lose Honey when she's just sixteen, not like this. You bring my daughter back to me John, and I don't care if you have to beg him on your hands and knees for forgiveness to do it."

“Why did you have to let him hit you?” Honey asked while breaking up ice cubes and emptying them into the plastic bag beside her. “What happened to Mr I can take on four grown men on my own?”

“Let me help with that,” I began, getting up.

“No, no you sit right there. I can manage,” Honey said hurriedly, she tied a knot in the bag and rushed back to the couch. “Lean back,” she coaxed gently and held the bag against my face.

“He’s your dad Honey, and he thought he was protecting you. I don’t blame him for getting mad. Frankly, I would have done a lot worse to anyone who I thought was taking advantage of you.”

“I don’t want you letting anyone hit you again,” scowled Honey angrily. “I don’t care who they are, and that includes my grandmother. If you can't fight offensive, then do it defensively.”

“Uh huh, I’ll try.”

“You’ll do more than just try or I’ll be jumping in,” she stated flatly. “I won’t stand by and watch you get hurt Azra.”

“Sooo anyway, I guess that you’ll be staying here then.” I say with the biggest grin on my face that my cut lip allows.

“If that’s ok, I'm sorry I didn’t get a chance to ask you it’s just…… OH,” Honey stopped when realization dawned and a smile bigger than mine appeared on her face.

Honey leaped at me, dropping the bag of ice cubes in the process.

“Ow, ow, ow,” I yelp.

“Ohmygosh I'm so sorry, are you ok?” Cried Honey, looking worried.

“I'm fine,” I smile as I got up, then pulled Honey to her feet. A second later I scoop her off the floor and she giggled as I carried her to my room.

I wake up rather suddenly the next morning. One second I'm asleep, the next I'm wide awake. My face feels like hell, and I have a massive headache, but all that disappears when I turn and see the most precious person in my world fast asleep beside me. I move slowly onto my side, the last thing I want to do is wake her.

I prop myself up on my elbow and stare at Honey, golden hair lying loosely across her face. And to think that she was worried about me seeing her that morning, how could she? She looks absolutely wonderful. I go to move the hair from her face then stop myself, but Honey must have sensed my movement because right at that moment her eyelids flicker and open. Honey looked at me and the smile I get from her is more radiant than the sun.

"Good morning," she yawned.

"Good morning beautiful," I reply.

Honey reached across my shoulder and pulled me towards her.

It's almost afternoon when we finally get out of bed.

"Have you got a spare toothbrush?" Asked Honey.

"I'll get you one," I nod while putting on my robe. I take another robe from the wardrobe and pass it to her, then head to the cupboard in the bathroom.

"Right, you have a choice of colours," I tell her, bringing back four toothbrushes.

"Is there a purple one?"

"Nope, sorry. Red, blue, white and yellow."

"Red," Honey replied, taking it from me.

"Is there anything you can lend me to wear? I don't think what I was wearing yesterday is going to be usable anymore." Honey pointed to the blood splattered clothes.

"Help yourself to whatever you want," I reply, nodding towards the wardrobe. "What's mine is yours."

She walked into the wardrobe and come back out five minutes later wearing a pair of sweatpants and a t-shirt that she knotted at her waist.

"They didn't ever look that good on me," I comment and get a smile in return. "Right, what are we eating coz I'm starving."

"What's our choices?" Asked Honey.

"We've got cornflakes, eggs, bread and baked beans. There's usually bacon but I finished the last of it a couple of days ago."

"I think we can manage something out of all that," laughed Honey, and we start preparing a late breakfast which we take then out to the balcony.

"So, what do you wanna do?" I ask between mouthfuls. "Should we go out or stay in?"

"Stay in definitely." replied Honey, sipping her tea. "Today's going to be our first full day together and I'd like to spend it here, with you."

We take our time eating, it's a beautiful day and the sun is out. There's a lovely view to the side of us, but all we have eyes for, is each other. All too soon the first meal we have ever made together is finished and we sat for a while with full stomachs just enjoying each other's company.

"The dishwasher's over here," I tell Honey when we finally go back in with our empty plates. Then we snuggle up on the couch and continue our conversation about what happened at her house last night. When I look at the time a little while later, we realise that we have been talking for over two hours.

"So, what should we do about dinner then?"

"What do you normally do?" Asked Honey.

"Paul does all the cooking, all I have here is breakfast stuff."

"Ooo, why don't we try making something ourselves?" Said Honey eagerly. "Come on, it'll be fun."

"Umm, ok." I reply hesitantly. "What should we make?"

"How about spaghetti bolognese?" She replied, getting into the idea. "It's supposed to be quite easy and it's one of my favourites," Honey announced excitedly. "Right, I'll look up the recipe and make a list of everything we need then we can go to the store to get the ingredients."

"I'll get some paper," I tell her, getting up and going to the study desk in my bedroom. "Call out what we need, and I'll make the list."

About forty five minutes later we're at the grocery store watching out trolly get filled with essentials that we hadn't put on the list.

"Do we really need potato chips?" Honey inquired, holding up two multipacks.

"Yeah, chuck em in."

"Which flavour?"

"If you can't decide, take em both. It'll get eaten," I reply. "And we need some more cola and bacon."

When we finally get to the checkout our trolly is bulging and we're wondering how the hell that happened.

"I'm paying for half that lot." Honey insisted.

"No, you're not, you're staying with me, so I get to pay. When I stay over at your place then you can pay."

"Like that's going to happen," she snorted.

"Well like I told you earlier, what's mine is yours so technically you are paying for half."

"Now you're playing word games," replied Honey.

"No." I say seriously as I take her hand and look into her eyes. "No games Honey, not between us. I meant what I said. Anyway," I turn back to our shopping. "I don't fancy carrying this lot home, and I don't really want to bother Paul, so it looks like a cab for us."

It takes us over half an hour to separate our ingredients and put the rest of the food away.

"Ok, boil some water and put the spaghetti in. Then drain the water when it's soft, sounds easy enough," Honey announced after checking the recipe again. She put a pan full of water on the cooker and turned it on.

"How brown should these onions be?" I ask, giving the pan beside her another stir.

"I'm not sure," Honey looked at them. "Give em another few minutes."

"Some of these onions are turning black and some aren't even properly brown," I warn about five minutes later.

"Just put the mince in then and mix it," suggested Honey while she put the spaghetti into the boiling water. "Emm Azra, half the spaghetti is sticking out of the pan. Are we supposed to break them before we put it in?"

"I don't know," I admit as I take a look. "It doesn't say anything about breaking the spaghetti," I tell her after checking the recipe.

"No its ok, look the bottom bit is getting soft and it's all going in now…what's that smell? Your mince is burning," Honey yelped, dashing over and stirring it. "Add some water, that should stop it burning."

"How much is a pinch?" I asked a few minutes later. "It says add a pinch of this stuff."

"I don't know, just take a bit between your fingers and put it in," Honey replied, looking at the recipe again.

"I already did that, twice, but it didn't look like anything actually went in."

"Then add some more," Honey suggested with a shrug.

"The spaghetti is overflowing." I yell ungently.

"Oh, damn." She shrieked. "What should I do Azra?"

"Empty some water out," I shout, running past to get a cup and handing it to her. "Maybe we should turn the heat down a bit.... Your phone's ringing."

"It's mum," Honey replied, looking at the screen. "Hi ma.... Yeah I'm fine.... uh huh, uh huh.... Yeah ok, we'll be there tomorrow about five. AZRA, the mince is burning again. Sorry ma gotta go, I'll see you tomorrow."

It took about an hour to finish cooking and we bring our dinner over to the dining table. The spaghetti seems to have solidified into one big lump, and we have to cut pieces off to serve it. I look at my plate and shudder. The spaghetti is like a brain that's just been dissected, and the Bolognese looks like some alien organism that could sprout legs and walk off my plate at any second. In fact, I'm starting to wish it would do just that, so that I wouldn't have to touch it. I look at Honey's hopeful smile, then back at my plate. She's expecting me to eat it.

My hand shook as I collect some mince on my fork and Honey's eyes widen. Don't chew just swallow, don't chew just swallow. I repeat as I bring the fork slowly up. My throat closes up when I put it in my mouth and the chair fell back as I jump up and rush to the sink, spitting the disgusting thing out on my way. I don't bother with a glass, I simply put my head in the sink and open the tap over my mouth.

"Oh God," Honey stammered, running over to me. "Are you ok?"

"Not really," I groan, washing my mouth, the water splashing all over my face and t-shirt "I can still taste it."

"I should have stopped you," Honey began. "I'm sorry, I just didn't think…." She started giggling.

"S'not funny," I moan between mouthfuls of water. "You didn't taste it."

"You should have seen the way you jumped out of the chair," Honey's really laughing now. "I thought you moved fast before."

"Let's see how fast you move when you taste it," I reply and start giggling as well.

A few seconds later we're both laughing our heads off.

"Pizza?" Honey suggested when she's able to talk.

"Pizza," I nod.

"I'll order it," Honey offered, walking to her phone, still giggling on the way.

Half an hour later the doorbell rang, and I collect our dinner.

"Finally," Honey moaned, she opened the box a bit and took a deep breath. "God that smells good, I'm starving."

The rumble from my stomach is an agreement to her statement and Honey giggled.

I take the box over to the large couch and set it between us as we begin to tuck in.

"So, what did your mum have to say?"

"She asked if we could come over," Honey replied, trying to eat and talk at the same time. "I told her we would tomorrow. Is that ok? We don't have to go if you don't want to."

"No, no. We should go. What do you think she's going to say? You told your dad you weren't going to come back till he apologised."

"Frankly, I don't care… Is it bad of me to hope he doesn't?"

I smile at that. "If he does, I replied. I think you should too."

"WHAT…NOO. He hit you, Azra. He had no right to do that, and I was perfectly justified to do what I did to help you."

"Yes, you were," I confirm, taking her hand. "But sometimes it's not just about right and wrong, sometimes both sides have to make allowances to move forward. And this time you're going to have to be the bigger person."

Honey huffed and continued eating her pizza quietly.

"Well, whatever happens, we still have at least one more night together." I whisper quietly and see her eyes lit up.

When I wake up the next morning, Honey's resting on her elbow looking at me.

"Morning," I yawn.

"You know," she replied. "I could definitely get used to this."

"Definitely," I echo, putting my arm around her waist and pulling her down towards me.

"So, what's the plan for today?" I ask as we cuddle.

"We stay exactly where we are for as long as possible, we order our food, and we don't go out till we're ready to meet my parents." Honey advised with absolute conviction.

"Works for me," I agree and snuggle up closer.

"Oh, and under no condition are you allowed in the kitchen again Azra…"

"Hey, now wait a minute," I interrupt her. "It wasn't just me in…." I pause there when I start to realise something. This might just work out for me in the long run, I think with a smile. "It's a bit harsh, but I suppose I see your point," I continue while trying not to grin.

"…. Until you learn how to cook," finished Honey.

Revelations

It's about ten minutes to five, Honey and I stand on the sidewalk and stare at her house.

"You know, I've gone in and out of this place all my life, but not once have I ever taken the time to actually stop and look at it," Honey mused thoughtfully.

"It's a bit of an unusual situation," I add softly.

It's a strange feeling," Honey continued. "Standing here, in front of my home… wondering if it is, in fact still My home."

"Of course it's your home," I assure her with a hug. "And no matter what happens next it will always be the house you grew up in."

"Well, shall we?" She finally urged, giving me a squeeze.

I nod and we slowly walk up the small path hand in hand.

Honey searched the small bag around her shoulders for her keys, there was a light jingle as she took them out and selected one, then paused.

"What's wrong?" I ask her.

"Umm, I just had a thought. After the way we left… well, I'm not sure if we should just walk in or knock first."

"Oh… yeah, good point." I agree. "Knock I think, it might be better if they let us in."

Honey slipped the keys back into her bag and lifted the metal knocker on the door, she held it for a few seconds before using it to tap gently. A few moments later the door opened, and her mum stood there. As soon as Mary saw Honey she grabbed her daughter in an embrace. Honey let go of my hand to hug her mum back.

"Are you ok?" Mary asked, releasing Honey and looking into her eyes.

"Uh huh."

Mary nodded then held Honey's hand as she led her in, Honey grabbed my hand and the three of us walk into the house holding onto each other. The tension we were feeling earlier lifted a bit as we went in. It's hard to remain serious with three people walking holding hands, especially with Honey having one arm stretched out in front holding her mum and the other stretched out at the back holding me. I feel a giggle come and cough to disguise it.

John was sitting at the dining table looking uncomfortable, and Mary finally let go of Honey to sit beside him. We take the opposite chairs, so Honey sat in front of her dad and I'm in front of her mum. There's absolute silence and the atmosphere turned a bit awkward as we all sit there not knowing where to look and none of us seem to want to catch anyone else's eye. Eventually, Mary cleared her throat rather pointedly and John looked down.

"I'm sorry I hit you," John mumbled, still staring at the table.

"Thank you sir," I reply. "It means a lot that you would say that."

I look at Honey, she seems to have found something of great interest to examine on the kitchen wall and refused to tear her attention away from it. I nudge her with my knee.

Whatever is on that wall seems to be far more captivating than I realise, and she totally ignores me.

I nudged her again.

"Quit it!" She snapped, her head turning to me then she sighed. "Sorry I hit you with a chair," Honey mumbled in the same volume and tone as her father had done a moment ago, her gaze now drawn down to the table top as well.

“Well,” I announce before I even realise what I'm doing. “Why don’t we all go out for dinner tonight and try to put this behind us. My treat of course.”

Honey stared at me with a “we didn’t discuss this look” and I shrug back lamely.

“I think that’s a great idea,” agreed Mary with gusto.

“Well, if we’re going out, I need to change,” stated Honey, getting up and taking my hand. “Come on Azra, you can help me pick out something to wear.”

Honey kept hold of my hand as she led me up the stairs and into her room. And as soon as we’re inside she slammed the door shut so loudly I almost jump.

“You think they heard that?” She asked with a smirk.

“I think your neighbours heard that,” I mutter.

“Good.”

“Sorry about the dinner thing, it just kinda came out.”

“It’s fine,” Honey assured me. “It’s not a bad idea actually, considering the tension down there right now, it's better if we’re all out of the house for a bit.”

“I’ll call Paul and see if he can come up with something appropriate.”

John looked up towards Honey’s room.

“She closed her door,” he announced.

“Yes, she did,” replied Mary.

“With him inside,” John stated flatly. “She’s not allowed to do that. Why did she do that? Should I go speak to her?”

"No, you shouldn't," answered Mary. "Our girl is growing up… faster than we want, but there it is. Honey went through hell when she broke up with Azra, and now that she has him back, she is absolutely devoted to him. Judging from the way he's behaved; I would say he feels exactly the same way about her."

Mary paused for few seconds to let her husband digest that.

"Any doubts or insecurities she may have had earlier have been burned away, and they've come together even stronger than they were before. Try and stop them now and they'll just roll over you. Get between them and you'll probably get crushed. The best we can do now if we want to be a part of their lives is to hold on tight and get dragged along."

John let out a little grunt, still staring at Honey's door.

"Mary took her husband's hand and led him to the sofa "Oh John, you should have heard Honey when I confronted her about… well, the pill. She was so confident of herself and her choices, there was a self-assurance in her voice that I'd never heard before. It wasn't quite appropriate to say so at the time, but I couldn't have been prouder of our daughter."

Thankfully Paul came through and found a place for us to go. The waiter led us to a circular table with a large candle in the middle and a low hanging bulb which was surrounded by an intricate shade. We all took a seat while he slid a menu in front of each of us. The place appears to have spent a lot on their ambience, because each table seemed to be a little island of light with the rest of the restaurant being quite subdued.

"Holy crap," cried John in shock after picking up the menu. "Look at these prices."

"Dad!!" Hissed Honey under her breath angrily.

"What? It's going to cost almost a fortnight's wages for us to have a meal over here." John turned to me in a huff. "I know your parents are rich, but they can't be ok with you throwing away money like this. And speaking of throwing away money, what the hell was that nonsense with you throwing away the necklace you gave Honey."

"Dad, that's enough." Hissed Honey again, although the tone of her voice seemed lost on her father.

"Leave it John," implored Mary.

"My parents are not rich sir." I tell him.

"What does that mean? Where...?? An inheritance, is that where the money comes from? That's even worse. You're spending money that someone else has spent a lifetime saving."

"I said that's enough dad," warned Honey, her voice low but no longer subtle. "You've got no right to judge Azra about what he does.

"It's not an inheritance sir, the moneys mine. I earned it."

"YOU...??" Stammered John, shocked. "How?"

"The stock markets. Trading stocks, shares at first. But it was when I started on crypto currency that things got really interesting. I'm very good with numbers sir."

Both of Honey's parents stare at me with their mouths open. I've never been happy at being the centre of attention and I look around uncomfortably. Honey squeezed my hand to reassure me, and I smile back to show how much I appreciate it.

"I think it's time you told us a little bit more about yourself son," whispered Mary.

"You don't have to say anything you don't want to," Honey assured me while staring pointedly at her parents.

I've told Honey everything about myself a while ago naturally. I look at her then nod at her parents. After a few seconds I raise my hand to call the waiter over and tell him what I want. Everyone else does the same and I use the time to get my thoughts in order.

Both pairs of eyes turn back to me as soon as the waiter walked away, and I cough to clear my throat.

"My parents are not rich, never have been." I began. "Quite the opposite actually. We lived in a small one-bedroom apartment and my bed was in a curtained off corner in our cramped living room. My father had two jobs and worked six, sometimes seven days a week. My mother worked as a cleaner for a small company, if you could call it that and she was always getting calls to work odd hours. Paul, my father's best friend and his wife helped out in any way they could, and I spent a lot of my younger years with them babysitting me. My parents hardly had any time for each other, but they still tried their best to make time for me. My favourite times were the few occasions when all three of us were together. You see, with the hours that they were working it didn't happen very often."

I reach across the table for the water and pour myself a glass, after taking a sip I continued.

"This was the way it had always been all my life and to me it was normal, I loved my parents, and they loved me. We didn't have much money, but we had each other. They could only afford the cheapest of everything, but they made sure that there was always food on the table. It was normal for me to get my clothes from second hand stores, and it was normal for me to keep wearing them till my arms and feet stuck out a bit. Naturally enough this did not go down well for me at school, and I was teased mercilessly for it."

"Are you ok?" Honey whispered.

I look at her and nod, it wasn't easy to talk about that and Honey knew it.

"It was a month or so after my thirteenth birthday when Paul, on a whim decided to tell me about the stock market and set up a virtual trading account for me. He explained that I couldn't actually make or lose any money on this type of account, it was only used to learn. Paul knew just how good I was in maths and said that he had been curious about this for a while. In the next few months I made more money than my father had in two years. When I showed him this, he and mum begged, borrowed and saved every penny they could to set me up with a proper trading account, although he had to have his name attached to it. Time with my parent was rare before, but during those months I hardly got to see either of them at all. Mum took on even more work and dad started taking on overtime on both his jobs. I got pretty used to living alone during that time."

The waiter arrived with our food and I pause while he put a plate in front of each of us. Honey finally let go of my hand to pick up her knife and fork, and I did the same.

"Paul's wife had been ill on and off for quite a while," I continued, as I pushed the food around my plate. "My parents finally sat me down and told me that it was cancer, it had been in remission but came back badly. They told me that the doctors had only given her a few more months to live. When she passed away Paul was devastated, they had no children and he simply gave up on life. He lost his job, his house, pretty much everything he had. It was our turn to help him and the first thing that we did with the money I was earning was buy a place and have Paul move in with us."

"Every few months I would take out half the money and put it in a savings account, reinvesting the other half. My father gave up one of his jobs and mum cut down on what work she took on. Eventually I had enough to insist that they didn't need to work anymore. My parents used to regularly talk about travelling while looking at brochures, planning where they'd like to go when they had the time, so with Paul's help I booked them on a world cruise."

Is that why you live alone? Asked Mary, and I nodded.

"Whenever one cruise finished, I would wait a bit before booking another. They didn't like leaving me, so I would have to book it without them knowing. I'd get the most luxurious ones then tell them exactly how much it had cost, and that we would lose the money if they didn't go. With the hard life we had, they didn't like to see any money go to waste, that made it easier to talk them into it."

"Do they live with you at all?" Asked John.

"The apartment that Paul lives in is theirs." I replied. "He stays there to act as my guardian when they're away. Paul told me that even before I was born, they had very little time for each other because of work. He explained that they would need time for themselves to learn to be a couple again."

I look at my barely touched plate, there's nothing really left I want to say so I make more of an effort to start eating. The rest of the meal is finished in silence.

It's been several months since the meal with Honey's parents, it's morning and I'm sitting on the edge of my bed looking at my bedside cabinet. I've been looking at it for at least half an hour now and my hand trembled when I finally open the top drawer. I slowly reach inside to take out the box from in it and a shiver went down my spine when I eventually find the courage to open it. How can something so small cause so much fear. I begin to shake and feel myself getting hotter and start sweating. Unable to hold it any longer I shut the box, throw it back into the cabinet and slam the drawer shut.

I've been looking for this for a while now, and ever since I found it a couple of weeks ago, I've been absolutely terrified. And I don't like being scared. My eyes get drawn to the cabinet every time I walk into my bedroom, and I've started to have trouble sleeping. For something so small its presence seems to have taken over the entire apartment.

No, I decide firmly. It has to be done, and I will do it. I take the box out again and quickly shove it into my jacket pocket, trying not to look at it. I'm already late and Paul will be waiting for me in the car by now, so I grab my bag and rush to the elevator. The journey down is tediously slow and I'm pacing left and right like a caged animal inside the tiny room while it crawls down. I start sweating again and when the elevator finally stops, I don't even wait for the doors to open properly before dashing out. My bag gets stuck, and I swear loudly startling the concierge as I pull it free.

Paul took one look at the state I'm in when I get in the car and knew exactly what I'm about to do.

"Are you sure you need to do this?" He asked solemnly.

I look at him dumbly for a minute then nod.

"Things are going great between the two of you right now," Paul continued, while snatching glances at me through the rear-view mirror. "There's no need to put everything at risk, maybe you should wait."

I take out a tissue and wipe my face and neck. I can't even speak so I just shake my head.

We arrive at Honey's house and Paul parked the car in the closest space he can find. I just sit in the back unable to move. After about five minutes Paul turned to look at me.

"Maybe today isn't the best time to do this."

"I've put it off long enough," I reply, forcing the words out before opening the car door and getting out. I start walking towards Honeys house. The closer I get the heavier my feet seem and the slower my steps become. When I eventually get to the front door, I look at it for a few minutes then back to the car.

Taking out another tissue I wipe my face again, and after a few minutes, press the doorbell.

"Good morning Azra," Mary said with a wide smile when she opened the door.

"Morning ma'am."

"Are you ok? You don't look well."

"F-fine, I'm fine." I stutter, walking in and head to the stairs. My heart is beating so hard, I can actually hear it and I'm sweating again. I run the back of my hand across my forehead as I approach her bedroom door.

Thoughts rush around and collide with each other, making a chaotic jumble in my mind and I struggle to find some firm ground in this earthquake inside my head. The little velvet box is in my hand again and I open it to look at the engagement ring inside.

Of course I love her, that much is indisputable. But why am I doing this? Why am I choosing this moment to propose? Is it simply because I love Honey? Or am I afraid of losing her again? And that I guess is the crux of my dilemma, the reason for my hesitation.

I realise that I may be about to do the same thing that Honey did when she broke up with me. I think I'm about to propose out of fear, I'm going to bind Honey to me not simply because I love her, but so that I won't lose her again. And there it is, for the first time since I started looking for this ring, everything makes sense.

Paul was right. I shouldn't be doing this, not yet, not for the wrong reasons. I close the box and put it back into my pocket. We have time, all time in the world and when I propose it will be because.....

The door opened and Honey stood there with a quizzical look on her face.

"I heard the doorbell ring ages ago," she said questioningly. How long have you been standing out here?

I stare at her dumbly.

"What's the matter? You look like you're about to faint." Honey said worriedly. ".... Azra? .... Azrael!!"

“I love you Honey,” I whisper finally as I wrap my arms around her.

“I love you more.” She replied.

My parents named me after an Angel, and I've often wondered why they chose that one. For only six letters I've always found the name too long and a bit extravagant. But hearing Honey say it that morning, it sounds just fine.

My name is Azrael, I'm sixteen years old and I am in love. Love, a simple four-letter word that’s powerful enough to change the course of the world. Yet words, for all their power, are not enough to encompass everything I feel for her. But if words are all that I have, then I would write a book, from the library in my heart.

THE END.

If the stars fell down

Out of the sky

Or the light of the sun went out

If the earth broke apart

Under my feet

I wouldn't even care

As long as I have you there

By my side.

S C Hughes

Please also try my book of poems, available now on Amazon.

The Depths Of Emotion

A Selection Of Poems

S C Hughes

Printed in Dunstable, United Kingdom

73030306R00092